The Cabbage Tree Creek Caper

A Novel by

JOHN DAVID SAYLES

ISBN: 978-1-923512-10-8 (Paperback)

A catalogue record for this book is available from the National Library of Australia

Cover Design: Liz Peters

Self-Published by John David Sayles with assistance by Clark & Mackay
Proudly printed in Australian by Clark & Mackay

Contents

Chapter 1

DAMNED IF YOU DO,
DAMNED IF YOU DON'T

On a Thursday evening at dusk, a Spanish-born skipper of a prawn trawler painted white, blue and yellow is standing on the deck of his pride and joy, the 'Santa Maria', moored at a dock in Sinbad Street, Shorncliffe. He is speaking on his mobile, "Yes boss… okay boss…we'll find out by tomorrow then… thanks boss." He turns to a German-born crew member sitting on the dock fixing a broken net. "No pickup tonight, Manny, but the boss says there will be something for you to collect tomorrow morning, so we should have a rendezvous in the bay over the weekend."

"Can ve just go out trawling tonight zen Tony?" Manny asks hopefully.

"If you want to Manny." He pauses and reflects. "You know, I wish we could go back to how it was before when we were just trawling for prawns like the good old days."

"Me too." Confirms Manny.

"But I am in too deep with these people, we both are. It all started when I owed them money and I thought if I did a few jobs for them and paid them off, that would be the end of it, but after the boss murdered… you know… the guy who didn't want any part of

7

it… and the boss ordered us to get rid of the body… well after that, we were in too deep, we are accessories to murder now, so…"

They are both now remembering that early morning a few years ago when they both restrained an errant crew member, who threatened to tell police what they were up to. The rebel spat in the boss's face, who retaliated by shooting him in the head, then after wiping the spittle of his face with a handkerchief, screwed it up and violently stuffed it into the dead man's mouth.

"I agree Tony," says Manny, "Okay zee extra money is nice, but I have a conscience, I am a fisherman first and I vould like to go back to how ve vere."

"So would I Manny, so would I. Okay, let's cast off and go and do what we love. And just wait and see what tomorrow brings shall we."

Chapter 2

AN IDYLLIC MORNING

The next morning, a giant cruise ship enters the Port of Brisbane at the mouth of the Brisbane River. The liner passes several huge industrial cranes that resemble a herd of skeletal giraffes galloping headlong into Moreton Bay to greet this new arrival at the port. The sea on the bay looks stunning as it shimmers like a million diamonds on the water's surface. At the same time, the grey outline of a Qantas jumbo jet can be made out high above the cruise ship as the 747 begins its slow descent towards the runway at Brisbane Airport. The aircraft gradually drops down behind the tree line of the Boondall Wetlands, close to Nudgee Beach until it is out of sight.

Taking all this in while sitting on his front porch in Jetty Street, Shorncliffe, Johnny Blakemore is relaxing with an early morning mug of tea cradled in his hands, while his pet greyhound, Misty, lays peacefully by his side. Shorncliffe is a quiet, old-fashioned North Brisbane suburb situated alongside Cabbage Tree Creek. The view from Johnny's home is Moreton Bay, whose Aboriginal name is Qandamooka, meaning people of the bay. A prawn trawler painted white, blue and yellow is cruising along the narrow channel by Baxter's Jetty into Cabbage Tree Creek, after a night out trawling on the bay. On the other side of the channel are dense mangroves that make up Dinah Island, claimed to be named after the wife of an early settler, who once lived there a long time ago. A pair of pelicans that always seem to hang around this area are moving along the channel and waiting expectantly for any fish scraps that might come their way. Johnny affectionately refers to these pelicans as P1 and P2.

Johnny is content living here. He is a professional actor and a pretty good one too. He always looks forward to returning home after being on location filming in another State or sometimes even in New Zealand. He is also very passionate about the local history of this area as he lives in one of the oldest houses still surviving, which originally belonged to Mr. Baxter. Tragically he had drowned underneath the jetty opposite in 1897 when his foot became trapped in the steps and couldn't free himself before the tide came in. It's been called Baxter's Jetty ever since.

The indigenous name for this area is Warra, meaning plenty of water. Dinah Island stretches from the waterfront on Moreton Bay to the junction of Nundah and Cabbage Tree Creeks and extends to Nudgee Creek. The Island was a sacred burial ground for the local Turrabul Tribe and the last recorded burial in 1892 was for King Johnny a Turrawn, meaning elder of the Turrabul. King Johnny was known as the King of Nudgee and once saved the life of one of the friendly European settlers whom he recognised during an ambush of the man while gathering his cattle. Johnny Blakemore swears that sometimes on a windy night, he can hear someone playing a didgeridoo on the other side of Cabbage Tree Creek, with the hypnotic humming sounds drifting across the inlet. However, none of his neighbours acknowledged ever hearing a similar sound. Reportedly the local Turrabul people had been badly treated by some settlers and police in the 1850s.

Since his wife Sarah passed from cancer four years ago, Johnny has lived alone, as his daughter Sophie is away at University in Canberra. While his wife was ill, he took a break from his acting career, to care for her full-time. He loved Sarah dearly and still feels the pain of losing her and is slowly but surely beginning to re-establish himself as an actor of some note by keeping busy learning scripts and acting on set, enabling him to momentarily take his mind off his loss. Before she became ill Johnny had toured

Australia in a stage play, John Buchan's "The 39 Steps" playing the leading role at venues in major Australian cities. He received rave revues for his portrayal of Richard Hannay, and he is featured regularly in TV commercials for a well-known Japanese car manufacturer. People often check him out but are respectful of his privacy, probably because they are aware of his sad loss. Johnny is 47 years old, 6 feet tall with handsome features, kind brown eyes and thick wavy light brown hair which is now starting to grey a little at the temples. Johnny is a much more vulnerable person than the tough characters he sometimes likes to create on film and stage. He keeps himself in shape by going swimming one day a week at the Sandgate Pool and when time allows, he manages a workout at a 24-hour gym right next door to the pool. Johnny's agent, Barbara Browning at "Plush Agency" in Brisbane, is very excited that he is now available for full-time to work again and is trying very hard to get him some regular roles in a "soapie" or other TV series, such as "Miss Fisher" or "Doctor Blake" or "Jack Irish" or "Harrow."

Johnny adopted his female greyhound, Misty after his wife died. He adores Misty, she has big brown doe-like eyes, is a beautiful cream colour, with white feet and has the most wonderful calm temperament, as most greyhounds tend to have. Misty has turned out to be a very good companion for him.

"Right then, Misty" says Johnny, picking up her leash, "Want to go for a walk?" Misty never refuses a walk, so he locks the house and puts Misty in the back of his red Daihatsu Terios.

"Let's go to the woods today girl, it looks like rain is forecast, so we'd better go now." He often talks to Misty.

Chapter 3

OFF TO THE WOODS

He drives out of Jetty Street and along the roads overlooking the foreshores of Shorncliffe and Sandgate, past his old school, St Patrick's College for Boys, known locally as St Pats. From Eagle Terrace Johnny can see that it's still low tide and the foreshore is looking like a myriad of tiny sand islands. At low tide, people can walk out a couple of hundred metres due east along the sand, before the sea is lapping at their feet.

Yes, Johnny love's living in this area, a very old-fashioned place, very slow paced; some say it has no pace at all. Sandgate and Shorncliffe have many unique characters including arty types, artists, poets, musicians and actors. Johnny has always had links with the local Sandcliffe Amateur Theatre Society, SATS for short and has been known to act in small cameo roles for them as a favour to the theatre president Daniel Colby, a close friend as they both attended the local public school and St Pats College in Shorncliffe.

After driving past other historical landmarks in Eagle Terrace, Johnny and Misty travel on through Sandgate, which has such a lovely village charm about it, with some buildings over a hundred years old. There's the Town Hall with its distinctive phallic-looking clock tower showing the time as 8:15 am and the chimes are playing as they do every fifteen minutes. Close by is the majestic old post office that is now a pub, The 4017, after the postcode for the area. When they arrive at their destination, the Third Lagoon Reserve in Brighton, Misty jumps out the back of the car and they make their way along to the track that will take them through the wetlands reserve. Here you can see recent Aboriginal paintings on tree stumps and fallen logs.

On these walks, Johnny often reflects on all the happy years that he and Sarah had spent together. They had been married 22 years when she died. Their daughter, Sophie, who is now 21 is studying Politics and International Relations at the University of Canberra. Johnny usually speaks to his daughter once a week by mobile phone to make sure she is okay. When Sophie does get back to Brisbane, she sometimes stays with old school friends but mostly prefers to go home to Shorncliffe to be with her dad.

Just then his phone rings, it's a call from his daughter Sophie,

"Hi Soppy." That is his nickname for her.

"Dad, I wish you wouldn't keep calling me by that childish name, I'm a big girl now."

"Sorry" he says, but he isn't, he loves to tease her, "How's things then, Sophie?"

"Well Dad, the reason that I am calling is to let you know that I will be coming back to Brissie next week, so do you think you can cope with me being home for a few days?"

"Sure thing," he says, "I've got no work lined up for a while, so it would be great to see you."

"Thanks Dad, look I just wanted to warn you in advance, you know, in case you had something planned, okay? Sorry but I gotta go now Dad, I have a class starting soon, love you, will call you again just before I leave Canberra to let you know what flight I am on, okay. Oh, and there is no need to pick me up from the airport, I'll catch the train to Shorncliffe station, okay? Bye Dad, love you."

"Bye Soppy, er sorry, I mean..." but she has already hung up.

Johnny and Misty are now on the other side of Third Lagoon Reserve and cross Bracken Ridge Road into the Deagon Wetlands Reserve. The trees here are all Paperbarks, a paperbark forest if you like. Here one can sometimes spot lorikeets, honeyeaters, possums, and fruit bats that feed on the paperbark flowers. Very occasionally one might see a red-necked wallaby in the bungwall ferns which are abundant here.

Johnny's phone rings again. This time it's a call from his agent, Barbara Browning from Plush Agency, "Hi Barbie, to what do I owe this pleasure?"

"Johnny, I have good news love, you have an audition for a feature film being shot on the Gold Coast. This is a supporting role, and it could give you some useful international exposure as well."

"Oh" says Johnny "Sounds interesting, when?"

"Next week, Tuesday, it's down at Village Roadshow, the usual drill, you know?"

"Yeah, that's great Barbie, thanks very much," says Johnny, "My daughter is coming home for a few days next week, she just rang actually, but I think I should be able to manage a half a day away from Shorncliffe."

"Super," says Barbie, "Look I will send you all the details by email, you know audition info, script etc..... you are going to look great as a pirate Johnny, speak to you soon."

"A pirate?" replies Johnny bemused, but Barbie has rung off.

"Well then, Misty, so much for a nice peaceful walk, eh girl? Better get a move on."

During the two phone conversations, they had continued along the track and are now approaching the Queensland Racing Training Track at Deagon. This is usually the limit of their walk as there is a loop that will return them to the car. Suddenly a flock of lorikeets flash past and Misty reacts by straining and tugging at her leash. She seems keen to leave the track as something seems to have taken her interest in a hollowed-out tree stump, just a few metres away. Johnny is cautious as he thinks there could be a snake curled up inside, but Misty is extremely interested in that tree stump. Johnny makes sure that the stump is not harbouring any snakes, but there is something inside glittering that catches his eye. The object is a small zip lock plastic bag, and he stoops down to pick it up. The small plastic see-through bag is of the type that can be re-sealed and when he inspects it more closely, he notices that there is a silver USB stick inside the bag.

"Good girl, Misty, aren't you clever, wonder how that got there, put there by kids eh…? Yeah, I bet you there's porn on this USB. We just made do with girly magazines when I was young," he laughs to himself as he remembers when he was a teenager and all the things he used to get up to.

Johnny places the small plastic bag into his jeans' pocket as drops of rain start to fall, bouncing off the bungwall ferns. The rain looks like it will be much heavier than was predicted in the weather forecast. From his back pocket, Johnny pulls on a dark blue coloured fold-up plastic anorak with a hood and puts it on while he continues walking Misty back to the track. He notices a man in a green hoodie about fifty metres away, who steps off the track to go behind a clump of paperbarks. Johnny assumes he must be going for a pee, so averts his gaze and walks past.

Misty is starting to get wet, so they pick up the pace and head back along the track to Bracken Ridge Road. As they wait for some cars to pass Johnny notices an unoccupied old blue Commodore in the local model airplane club's car park, but no one is operating any flying objects at the present time.

When they cross the road, coming from the opposite direction is Phillip with his greyhound Krystal, who is a similar cream colour to Misty. The greyhounds look like two peas in a pod and Phillip is wearing an almost identical coloured anorak as the one Johnny is wearing.

"Snap" says Phillip and they both laugh.

Johnny and Phillip often cross paths when they are out walking their greyhounds in this area and always stop for a chat when they do. But because the rain is getting heavier, today is not a day for a conversation, so they say their goodbyes and part company. By the time Johnny and Misty get back to the car the rain has eased slightly, so it was just a passing shower after all. Johnny puts his hand in his jeans pocket fiddling for his car keys and can feel the small plastic bag his pet has just found. He loads a bedraggled-looking Misty into the back of the car and places the bag containing the USB stick into the car's dashboard compartment, with the intention of checking it out later.

He drives back to Sandgate, parks in the Ibis Shopping Centre underground car park and does a quick shop of bread and milk. At the supermarket's checkout, he bumps into his good friend Danny Colby. "Hi Cheezer," says Johnny, Cheezer is Dannys nickname from school for obvious reasons, "How's things with you, is Christopher still on holiday in Europe?" Christopher is Danny's son.

"Yeah mate, he's just taking a year off before he starts University, I think he's in Scandinavia somewhere at the moment, oh to be a twenty-year-old again, eh?"

"Yes, especially in Scandinavia."

"Anyway Blakey," that's Johnny's schoolboy nickname, "I'm glad I bumped into you, I was going to ring you about going out tonight. A few of us are meeting up at the 'Unplugged Cafe', you know, first Friday of the month, Mandy's going too." 'Unplugged Café' is a popular event in Sandgate, held at the local community centre on Rainbow Street, where local musicians and comedians entertain for no fee. You never know what you might get to see there, as the acts are sometimes a bit inexperienced, but at other times quite brilliant, none-the-less it is always a wholesome fun night out.

"I hear that they have a great lineup tonight and top of the bill are The Gypsy Blues Band who are supposed to be quite good. As an extra treat, they have a burlesque dancer with them." Danny looks at Johnny expectingly.

"A burlesque dancer? Now that does sound interesting Cheezer," Johnny quips back with a smile on his face. "Yeah, why not, yeah, I will see you there. Sorry cannot hang around, mate, Misty's in the car, but we will talk later okay, and you can tell me all about your next play at SATS."

"Oh, yes it's going to be brilliant," says Danny "It's a comedy, an English farce, lots of doors opening and closing and misunderstandings with wives and scantily dressed girlfriends and guys whose pants fall down."

"Aren't most of your plays pretty much like that" says Johnny.

“Yeah! I suppose they are mate” replies Danny. They both laugh and part company.

Chapter 4

MAN IN A HOODIE

A short stocky unshaven man in a grey anorak has left his blue commodore parked in the model airplane car park on the edge of the Deagan Wetlands. He is about to perform an important errand; one he has done on multiple occasions. His task is to pick up a vital piece of information that will provide details of an important rendezvous. The man is walking along a path in the Deagon Wetlands and makes his way to a walking track. Rain is beginning to fall so he zips up his anorak and covers his head with the hood. Before too long he spies a man with a cream-coloured greyhound on a leash. Noticing the man with the dog is putting on a navy anorak due to the rain, the hooded man is concerned they are standing close to where he needs to collect his information from. He assumes they must have momentarily left the track because the dog needed to relieve itself. So, being cautious as he does not want to be spotted by them, he leaves the track and hides behind some paperbark trees to observe what this man and his dog are up to. He waits a short while until they have passed and are completely out of sight. Then, when he is certain no one else is around, he emerges from behind the paperbarks and walks towards a hollowed-out tree stump and stoops to look inside.

"Was zum teufel?" exclaims the man as he puts his hand inside the tree stump, and after feeling around removes it empty handed. He stands there with a puzzled look on his face, then the realisation of what may have happened sinks in. He tugs his hood as far over his face as he can and walks briskly along the track. He desperately needs to catch up with the man and his dog and confront them. When he rounds the bend in the track, he sees a man in a navy anorak with a cream-coloured greyhound on a leash walking towards him, but they suddenly turn around and go back towards Bracken Ridge Road. It is now starting to rain even heavier than before and the man in the hoodie picks up a piece of a dead branch lying on the ground and says to himself, "Ich stecke in der scheisse." He starts running towards the man in the navy-blue anorak and strikes him from behind with the piece of wood, catching him across his right temple. Phillip falls to the ground still holding on to Krystal's leash. The man in the hoodie starts rummaging through Phillip's anorak and trouser pockets saying "Wo is das? Where is it, where is it?"

"Where is what?" cries out Phillip who is still lying on the ground in pain "I don't have any money on me, I'm just walking my dog for Christ's sake!" The man in the hoodie attempts to strike Phillip again, prompting Krystal to nip the assailant's backside and causing him to cry out "Swinehund." Krystal growls and barks at his master's attacker who is raising his hand holding the piece of wood and is about to strike the dog when he becomes aware of the traffic on Bracken Ridge Road. He is afraid someone will see what is happening and leaves the scene as quickly as possible. He looks a sorry sight as he runs back to his car, with one hand on his backside trying to cover a large tear in his trousers.

Phillip is now struggling to get to his feet, and staggers towards Bracken Ridge Road while still holding onto Krystal's leash, he struggles to get too far before collapsing to the ground. A passing motorist noticing that Phillip is in distress, pulls his car onto the side of the road and sprints to Phillip's side to offer some assistance.

Chapter 5

THE BOSS RECEIVES BAD NEWS

On Friday afternoon an anxious-looking Manfred Muller wearing a grey hoodie is walking along Sinbad Way and nervously approaches the 'Santa Maria,' as he is very concerned that he doesn't have the item that the Basque man, Tony Pesaro, is expecting.

Tony notices Manny and says, "Hi Manny, where's the commodore?"

"Had trouble starting it Tony, came on the train today." He hesitates, then says slowly, "Err Tony, I have zum bad news for you."

"What do you mean Manny?" replies Tony sternly.

The little package zat I usually pick up in ze voods, it's not zere, maybe zey forgot to put it zere. Maybe zere's no job zis month."

"Maybe you are just an idiot Manny," Tony replies curtly, "Of course they left it there, the boss told me last night that it was ready to be picked up this morning because we are expecting the date, time and place of our next pick up to be confirmed."

"Vell, I'm sorry but it vas not zere, Tony."

"Well, where could it be then?" retorts the Spaniard losing his temper "Look everything always works like clockwork. Someone always leaves it in the hollowed-out tree trunk, then they report to the boss that the drop has been made. Then the boss tells us to collect it so we can give it to him. Only we know where to collect it from, even the boss has no idea where the collection point is.

Everybody involved in this has their own small part to play, just so there's no hiccups, so nobody can take over the whole operation. Do you understand me, Manny?"

"I zink I know who took it!" blurts out the German.

"What do you mean, you think you know?"

"Just before I got to ze tree trunk, I saw zis man valking his hund nearby, he must have tuk it."

"Why didn't you follow him, when you thought he might have taken it?"

"Vell, I did follow him Tony, zen I hit him on the head and knocked him down vile ve vere still on de edge of the voods, but zere vas nothing on him, zen his hund bit me on the arse and ve vere near a road and I vas scared someone might see me, so I had to get out of zere very fast."

"Fuck Manny, do you know how much trouble we are in now? These people are not playing games, you know, the stakes are too high."

"Sorry Tony, but it vos not my fault, it vas not in the tree trunk."

"Maybe not Manny, but they don't see things that way, I'm going to have to tell the boss straight away."

He picks up his mobile phone and after pondering for a few seconds, he dials a number. The call is answered almost immediately by a person with an educated voice, "Tony! It is usually for you to ring me, is everything in order?"

"No, boss, it's not, sorry to ring you, but we do have a problem, err Manny went to collect the item as usual this morning and it wasn't there."

"I'm going to pretend you didn't say that Tony... what do you mean, it wasn't there?"

"We think someone has accidentally come across it in the woods, a guy walking his dog."

"Oh no, that moron Manny hasn't been doing silly things has he."

"What do you mean boss?"

"I just heard a news item on the radio. It seems there has been a mugging in the Deagon Wetlands, a man wearing a grey hoodie bashed a man walking his greyhound. Does that sound like anyone we might know?"

"Erm, yes, boss, Manny thought this dog walker had taken it and tried to get it back off him. He even went through his pockets, but the man's dog bit him so he ran away, he was afraid that someone might have seen him."

"Someone might have seen him. Of course he has been fucking seen and with all the cctv nowadays they will quickly work out it who it was, won't they?" He pauses, "Alright, okay, listen to me, this man with the dog has been taken to hospital, I'll pay him a visit and hopefully get it back."

"Oh, that's great boss, shall we go out tonight as per usual?"

"Oh yes, just go out as per usual Tony, but one more thing?"

"Yes boss."

"Tell me, does Manny have his car with him?"

"No boss, engine trouble I think, he left it at home today."

"That is good, one less thing to worry about. Look, Tony, I want you to sort out the Manny problem, do you understand what I am saying?"

Tony pauses, "But boss, what do you mean, I couldn't do that… what are you asking me to do exactly?"

The boss is now incredibly angry, "Never mind, you useless piece of shit, I will send Ronny to crew with you tonight. He will know what needs to be done and I will inform you later if the pickup is on tonight or another night. Then you will receive the necessary coordinates." The phone goes dead.

"Vot did he say?" asks Manny who has a worried look on his face.

"Err… he said he would sort everything out, Manny, and he'll let us know when the pickup is going to be, so don't worry. Oh, and he is going to send Ronny to crew with us tonight, so let's get everything ready so we can leave when he gets here." Tony closes his eyes and makes the sign of the cross.

Chapter 6

NEWS OF A BASHING

That evening, on the Five O'clock News, Johnny's ears prick up on hearing a TV news report.

"There has been a mugging in the Deagon Wetlands this morning. A sixty-year-old man walking his dog has been assaulted by an unknown attacker who bashed him about the head." There is news footage showing an ambulance leaving the scene at Bracken Ridge Road and a uniformed police officer with a cream greyhound on a leash.

"The man has been concussed slightly, and his dog is being looked after by some of his neighbours."

"Krystal!!" shouts Johnny.

The report continues "Because of head injuries sustained, the victim has been taken to the Redcliffe Hospital for observation. Anyone who was in the vicinity of Bracken Ridge Road near the Deagon Wetlands at around eight thirty this morning and who may have seen anything are urged to ring Crimestoppers immediately."

Johnny decides to ring the Sandgate Police Station straight away and when he gets through, asks to speak to Sergeant Michael Murphy, an old school colleague from St Patrick's College. In fact, in their teens, Johnny, Danny and Mike were known as the 'Three Musketeers,' and they were very close friends. Luckily Spud, as he was known at school, is on duty and Johnny advises him that he had spoken to the man who was bashed while they were both walking their dogs in the wetlands that morning and that the only other person he saw was a thick-set short man, wearing a grey hoodie which was pulled down to cover his face, so it doesn't enable him to give the police sergeant a detailed description of what the man looked like. Johnny also mentions the blue commodore car parked nearby, and that he had not taken a note of the number plate. Mike thanks him for his call and gives Johnny his mobile phone number just in case he remembers anything further and tells him not to bother ringing the police station again. Because they are old mates, Mike says just ring him directly on his mobile and he'll deal with it personally and adds that he will be in contact when he has found out anything further.

Johnny decides to go round to the Redcliffe Hospital straight away as he is concerned about Phillip's injuries. He puts Misty on the back porch and drives to Redcliffe, via the Houghton Highway over the bridge linking Brighton with the Peninsula. Parking his car, Johnny enters the hospital and goes directly to the reception desk, but it suddenly dawns on him that he does not know Phillips' surname. Although they often cross paths when walking their greyhounds, they only know each other by their first names and have never enquired much about each other's private lives at all. The main topic of conversation between them was always greyhound behaviour. He is not even sure if Phillip knows he is an actor as his occupation has never come up in any of their conversations. The receptionist advises Johnny that Phillip is in the West Ward on the 6th Floor and that his surname is Simpson. He is waiting to catch a lift to the desired floor, as a patient is being wheeled by in a bed, and he suddenly becomes emotional. This is the hospital where his wife passed away in the palliative care unit, and it is the first time that he has returned here since that tragic night. He is deep in his thoughts as the lift doors open and he stands back to let a few people get out, including a tall well-built bald man in a black suit who reeks of cologne. On arriving at the West Ward reception desk, the young nurse asks if he is a relative and Johnny explains that Phillip only knew him as Johnny and his cream greyhound as Misty.

She asks him to wait and after speaking with Phillip, the nurse advises "He would be happy to see you now, Mr. Blakemore." So, it does seem Phillip is fully aware of his casual friend's identity after all. Johnny follows the nurse to a room where there are only two patients, and she indicates Phillip's bed to him. In the other bed is a male patient with his leg raised in the air, who has a middle-aged female visitor sitting at his side.

The nurse appears a little flustered in her manner recognising the actor that Johnny is. "Would you like a cup of tea Mr. Blakemore?" she says smiling sweetly and looking at him admiringly, "It wouldn't be any bother."

"Oh no thank you," says Johnny, "It's very kind of you though."

She smiles again "Just let me know if you need anything then, Mr. Blakemore" and leaves the room.

The middle-aged lady visitor sitting alongside the other bed turns her head sharply, giving the nurse a withering look as she leaves, suggesting she is offended, as a cup of tea was not offered to her.

Johnny finds a spare chair and quietly draws it up to Phillip's bedside. His casual friend is sitting up in bed with a few pillows supporting him and his eyes are closed. Observing Phillip, Johnny agrees that as the news bulletin mentioned he does look about sixty years of age with his grey hair. Sensing someone is now close by, Phillip slowly opens his eyes and then peers at his visitor. Johnny thinks he looks a little worse for wear, but not too bad considering his ordeal. "Hi Phil mate, I heard what happened and thought I'd come round and check that you're okay." Phillip is trying to raise a smile, "Well then, what happened to you mate?"

"I'm not sure, Johnny," says Phillip, whose right eye closes each time he attempts to speak, the injury is obviously causing him a great deal of pain.

"Did this happen shortly after I saw you this morning?"

"Well, yes mate it did, just after I saw you and Misty near Bracken Ridge Road, the rain started to get heavier, so I decided not to go any further along the track, and we turned back around to go home to Brighton. Soon after, I felt this pain on the side of my head," he puts his hand to his bandaged right temple, "And the next thing, I'm sprawled on the ground and my head is spinning. This guy wearing a grey hoodie was on top of me, feeling inside my pockets and he says, where is it, where is it? in some kind of foreign accent. I says to him, where is what!! I haven't got any money with me, I'm just walking my dog. Then Krystal nipped him on his bum, and he shouted, you swine hound. I think that's what he said, because he had a funny accent, then he ran off and not long after, I heard a car start up and speed off. I think he was worried because we were close to Bracken Ridge Road, maybe he was scared that he might be seen by someone driving past."

"Did you happen to see the car that drove off," enquires Johnny.

"No mate, my head was spinning, after a while I did manage to get back onto my feet and I was able to stumble along for a few more yards while keeping a hold of Krystal's leash of course. I think I must have passed out and fell to the ground again, don't remember that too clearly. After a while, a passing motorist must have seen me on the ground and stopped to help me and after I came round, I was able to tell him what had happened. He was a god send because he quickly phoned for an ambulance and the police."

"Would you be able to recognise this man that attacked you, Phil?"

"No, no idea Johnny, I really didn't get a very good look at him because of the hood pulled down over his face."

Johnny lets Phillip know that he also saw a man in a grey hoodie, and he would not be able to recognise him either, but he has already advised the police about everything he could remember. Johnny gives Phillip his mobile telephone number and says if he needs any assistance with anything, just to give him a call. He also gets Phillip's home address and the details of the neighbours who are looking after Krystal. He suggests that maybe he could take both dogs for a walk sometime while Philip is in hospital. Phillip assures Johnny that it won't be necessary as he expects to be discharged from the hospital the next day.

Johnny also inquires if any of Phillip's friends or relatives have been to see him, as he knows Phillip is also a widower.

Phillip says, "Oh yes, my son, his wife and two grandchildren were all here this afternoon. They went home at 5:30pm, and a little while ago a plain-clothed police detective turned up to ask some questions. And you know what, he didn't leave that long ago, in fact he left just before you arrived Johnny."

"A police detective… for a mugging, with nothing stolen, that sounds unusual," says Johnny.

"Yes, that's what I thought too," says Phillip, "I told him that I'd already told the uniformed police everything that I could remember, but he seemed to be more interested in wanting to know what part of the Deagon Wetlands that I had been walking Krystal in this morning and also asked if I had I found anything whilst I was there."

"Really?" says Johnny, now remembering the USB stick that he found in the hollowed-out tree trunk.

Phillip continues, "But I told him that I didn't get very far into the wetlands, as it was starting to rain heavily. I also told him that I saw you and that we both had a laugh about us wearing similar coloured plastic anoraks and having greyhounds that were both a cream colour. Oh yes, he seemed to be most interested in that all right."

"Oh really," says Johnny, "Did you tell him anything else?"

"Just your name and that you are well known around here, because of your acting and everything, and that you live in Shorncliffe somewhere. After that, he didn't ask me any more questions about the mugger at all, just wanted to make sure that I hadn't found anything. Maybe he'll contact you as well, Johnny?"

"Yes, maybe he will Phil," says Johnny "By the way, what was this detective's name?"

"Do you know," says Phillip "Now I think about it, I don't remember him telling me his name, in fact I don't even remember him showing me his badge either, is that unusual?"

Not wanting to alarm him Johnny laughs and responds, "I think you've been watching too many American cop shows Phil." But having played many police roles in his time, Johnny knows the drill when asking witnesses questions. He also fancies that he would have made a good Detective Inspector himself, well in TV and films anyway. He is also a little intrigued by this mysterious detective who visited the hospital.

"What did this detective look like Phil?" Johnny asks casually, "You know, so I might be able to recognise him, just in case he turns up on my doorstep to ask me a few questions as well."

"Oh, of course mate, no problem." He thinks for a few seconds, closing his right eye slightly. "Well, I reckon he's about 6' 2" tall, he had cold grey eyes, and he wore a very smart black suit, about 40 years old I reckon. A very fit looking bloke he was, oh yeah, and he was bald." Phil pauses and adds "And he had a strong smell of cologne, overpowering it was, I didn't like him."

Johnny considers what he has said, "Bald, tall, black suit, smelt of cologne... Phil did you say that this err... this detective, has only just left?"

"Yeah mate, about five minutes before you arrived," says Phillip.

"Oh really," replies Johnny, who is now remembering the bald man getting out of the lift who reeked of cologne. "Phil, can you remember anything else at all about this detective?"

"Well yes I do" says Phillip, whose right eye is now almost fully closed.

"And what's that Phil?"

"He was a Pom, and he talked very posh."

Johnny chuckles, "Okay, you take care mate," and leaves.

When Johnny arrives home, he remembers what Phillip had told him about the police detective being more interested in where he had been in the wetlands and what he may have found, rather than asking him questions about the mugger. He retrieves the USB stick in the plastic bag from his glove box, and when he loads it up into his laptop computer, he is disappointed. Not because it does not contain any porn as he had initially thought it would, but because there is just a series of numbers and letters that don't mean anything to him at all.

06/07.02:58.1.88.27.3365S.153.2502E

However, he decides to save the information into a file on the computer and copies the details onto a piece of paper which he folds in half and puts inside a first edition of a Charles Dickens' novel that he has been re-reading, but he neglects to eject the USB from the computer.

Johnny then decides to ring Sergeant Mike Murphy again on his mobile to advise him of the mysterious detective who had been to visit Phillip in the hospital.

His call is answered almost immediately, and Johnny says "Hi Spud, just wanted to advise you that I visited Phillip Simpson in hospital this evening, you know, the man who was mugged this morning near Bracken Ridge Road. Well, he told me that a police detective had been there to see him and asked him a few questions. And the questions seemed to be a bit strange, like he wanted to know if Phil had found anything in the woods? Phillip also gave him my name as I had been walking my dog in the woods at the same time and he also told him that we have similar looking greyhounds."

"Really and err... did he?" says Mike.

"Did he what, Spud?" replies Johnny confused.

"Did he err... did Mr. Simpson find anything?"

"Well, he told the detective he didn't."

"And did he tell you he didn't find anything?"

"Yes mate," replies Johnny slightly irritated, "As I said, he didn't find anything."

"Did you err..." there is a short pause before Mike continues," I mean... did the detective give Mr. Simpson his name?"

"Well, that's just it," says Johnny, "No he didn't provide Phil his name or even show him any ID."

"That's very unusual," says Mike "But maybe Mr. Simpson might have been a little confused, what with the knock on his head and everything. And the detective would have been aware that uniformed police had already asked him relevant questions about the mugger... err... any idea what he might have looked like?"

"The detective? Well yes," says Johnny and gives him a description as per Phillip's account and from his brief encounter he had by the hospital lift, which was only from a rear view.

"Oh, and Phil said he had a British accent," added Johnny. "That should make it a lot easier for you to locate him mate, I can't imagine that we have too many Pom detectives in the Queensland police force, do we Spud?"

"Well, I couldn't really say for sure Johnny, I don't know them all, anyway as I said because of Mr. Simpson's knock to the head, he may have been a little confused about someone having an accent." Mike pauses, "And remember, he thought the attacker had an accent as well, didn't he?" Mike pauses again, "So everything he heard was probably confusing to him, look mate, just leave it with me eh and I'll check it all out, I'm about to knock off now, so I'll ring you tomorrow, and remember, there's no need to speak to anyone else about this, I'll deal with it, okay?"

"OK Spud, no worries…. oh, one more thing," Johnny is now looking down and touching the USB that is still in his computer.

"Yes," says Mike.

"Err… oh it's nothing mate," says Johnny, now having second thoughts, "Oh and Mr. Simpson said he heard a car drive off just after he was bashed, you'll check out that commodore I mentioned to you before won't you."

"Of course, Blakey, I'm right on it."

'Great, speak to you soon Spud," and hangs up the phone.

Johnny now decides to check out his emails on the computer. There is one from Barbie at 'Plush Agency,' with all the details for his audition with Disney at Roadshow Studios on Tuesday, with an attached script to learn.

"Hey this is the next Pirate film," he says enthusiastically to Misty, "Barbie knew I would be up for this, it would be so cool to be involved in."

He glances at the script and practices in his best pirate voice, "Shiver me timbers… I'll 'ave ye walking the plank ye scurvy rats… get ye up them yardarms ye lazy scum!! Ha ha, eat yer heart out Cap'n Sparrow arrrrrrrrrggghhh!!"

He is interrupted by his mobile phone ringing; Daniel Colby is calling him, and Johnny immediately knows why.

"Cheezer, shit... you are at 'Unplugged Cafe' aren't you?" suddenly remembering his promise to meet him there.

"Yes," says Daniel "Did you forget? We are all here, Mandy," that's his wife, "And other people you know, everyone's very keen to see you, it's been a long time for some."

"Sorry Cheezer, but I've had an interesting sort of day, it completely slipped my mind, what time is it?" He glances at his wristwatch, "Damn it's seven thirty, I'll be there as quick as I can."

"Okay, just hurry up and get here mate, got a surprise for you, see ya," Danny rings off.

"Surprise?" thinks Johnny, "He's already told me about the burlesque dancer, oh he must have forgot," and rushes to have a shower and get himself ready to meet up with his friends.

UNPLUGGED CAFE

After a shower and a shave, Johnny changes into a clean shirt and glances at the print of a John Williamson painting on the bedroom wall. It is "The Lady of Shalott" a famous painting representing the ending of Alfred Lord Tennyson's poem of the same name. The painting reminds him of the end of his wife's battle with cancer. The young woman depicted in the painting does resemble his wife Sarah with her pale features and long auburn hair. His wife did love the poem by Tennyson, so he is feeling a little sad now thinking that maybe he is not in the right frame of mind to be going out and having a fun time with friends. But he pulls himself together and decides he must attend, because after all he did promise that he would be there, so he had better not let Danny and the rest of them down. He puts Misty on the back porch, locks up the house and heads for his car parked alongside in the street. He does not notice a puff of vape smoke coming out of a green Mini Cooper parked only a few metres away down Jetty Street. He drives the short distance down Friday Street and arrives at Rainbow Street and the Community Centre where 'Unplugged Café' is being held. On the way there he hears another report about the mugging on his car radio "There are reports of a man wearing a grey hoodie being in the woods at the same time the mugging took place and Police would like to speak to anyone who owns a blue commodore which was parked in the vicinity."

"Good on you Spud," shouts Johnny aloud.

Johnny parks opposite the community centre and crosses Rainbow Street, just after noticing a green Mini Cooper has come from the same direction as himself. The car passes him, does a U-turn and heads back towards Shorncliffe. Johnny is more interested in the sound of a guitarist's music coming from inside the building, who's playing Bob Dylan's classic song 'Like a Rolling Stone,' not the best rendition. Not that Johnny minds though, he admires anyone who can get up on a stage and have the guts to perform, whether it be acting, singing, playing music, dancing or stand-up comedy and everyone performing tonight is not in it for the money. They are volunteering their services because they love what they do.

Johnny pays the five-dollar entrance fee to Jenny, a pleasant plump middle-aged lady showing off plenty of cleavage and attending the front desk in the hall outside the music room. He enters the noise-filled room, orders a beer at the bar then joins Danny and the others at a large circular table where they have saved him a seat. There's the Colby's, Danny and his wife Mandy, a bright and bubbly lady in her forties with shoulder length wavy blonde hair. They are both sporting big smiles, as they are so pleased that Johnny has decided to join them. Also seated are a genial middle-aged French-Canadian couple, Guy and Amelie Boudreaux, who are both wearing colourful Hawaiian-style shirts. Guy, a short lean-looking man and his petite wife Amelie are probably the theatre group's biggest fans, attending almost every production and often making generous donations at fundraising events. The Boudreaux's reside on a thirty-four-metre luxury yacht, 'Acadian,' which they named because of their roots. The yacht, which they sailed across the Pacific several years ago, is moored in the Sandgate Yacht Club Marina. Then there is the obvious surprise that Danny mentioned, it's Cherie O'Bryan, who often plays the female lead in many of Danny's plays. Cherie is a particularly attractive woman aged in her late thirties, about five foot, six inches tall, with short raven-coloured hair and piercing blue eyes. Cherie is dressed in slacks and a tight-fitting cashmere jumper which shows off the curvature of her ample breasts. Apart from those sitting at their table, there is the usual crowd. Drawn to Johnny's attention is a tall skinny guy with sharp features wearing a top hat and a 'Where's Wally' striped T-shirt. The strange character never sits at a table but always stands taking up certain poses as if he is a Marcel Marceau mime artist, like the bass player who was in the Skyhooks Band. With him is his wife or maybe girlfriend, heavily made up with long eyelashes and mascara. She is wearing a long black lacy dress, a string of pearls around her neck and a pink knitted beret. Her look reminds Johnny of Bonnie Parker from the film 'Bonnie and Clyde.' Marcel is standing immediately behind her whilst they sway rhythmically to the beat of the music. Bonnie occasionally flings her arms up in the air in an arc like a flamenco dancer and does a pirouette whilst never moving more than a couple of inches away from him.

There is a rail line at the rear of the community centre, it runs between Sandgate and Shorncliffe Stations and every fifteen minutes an electric train sounds a toot and rumbles past. At Shorncliffe, the trains terminate and then return to Brisbane and beyond. There is always a crowd of people sitting out on the back deck, a designated area for the smokers who only seem to venture into the main room when they feel the need for refreshments. There is always a variety of tasty food available, which is cheerfully dished up by volunteers. The menu usually includes soup of the day, a variety of pasta and mince dish or a mild curry with rice, and for dessert, apple pie or pavlova, all at a reasonable cost.

The guitarist, who is dressed in jeans, a red and white check shirt, a leather jacket, Cuban heeled boots and an Akubra hat, is now playing his last number; a Monkees song, 'Last Train to Clarksville' that seems appropriate as another train as if by cue is now rumbling past at the rear of the building. It is difficult to talk while an act is playing music, although much of the audience continues to do so. Johnny likes to show a little respect to the people who have come here to entertain everyone by not talking during their set and enjoying the music.

As the guitarist's rendition of his final song ends the emcee, a jolly looking man in his fifties jumps onto the stage and asks everyone to "Give it up for Dusty Boots," the musician.

Danny then turns to Johnny saying, "So Johnny, I think you know everyone here." In response, Johnny smiles while acknowledging everyone at the table. Danny goes on to say, "I also bumped into Guy after seeing you this morning and when I told him that you would be here, he was keen to come and bring his wife Amelie along." They both nod and smile at Johnny.

"How have you been lately, Johnny?" asks Mandy politely.

"I'm good, really good." Johnny knows they are still sad about his loss of Sarah, passing so young, even though it has been a few years now.

Cherie is knocking back a glass of white wine while looking intently at Johnny who averts his eyes, struggling not to look at her breasts. He is wondering if she is wearing a bra underneath that cashmere jumper but then smiles and looks her square in the eyes; and beautiful blue eyes they are too. Johnny suspects, no not suspects, he knows that Danny has asked Cherie to come along so she could be good company for him. It has been a while since his wife died and he had loved Sarah so much, but he still does not feel ready to date anyone yet.

"Yeh, I'm fine thanks," says Johnny, putting on a brave front. "Anyway, how long have you guys been here drinking, you all look pissed," he laughs.

"Since seven o'clock," says Cherie accusingly, "So you'd better begin to start catching us up."

"Okay, I will," says Johnny looking down at his empty glass slightly bemused, "I suppose it's my shout then, what's everyone having?"

Danny, Mandy, and Cherie respond with their requests. Guy and Amelie, who each still have a large red wine in front of them, decline by saying they might get another drink when they have finished the ones they have.

While Johnny is at the bar getting in his designated shout of two beers and two white wines, he notices that Marcel and his girlfriend Bonnie have gone outside to the front of the building, presumably to smoke between acts. Just as he is trying to figure out how he is going to transport the drinks back to the table, Cherie arrives by his side. "I thought you might need a hand, Johnny," she pauses "With the drinks I mean," she giggles.

"Oh yes thanks," Johnny hesitates, "So, how are things with you? I have not seen much of you since that play you did about four years ago, 'Up Pompeii,' wasn't it? You played Suspenda didn't you?"

"Yes, that's right, Suspenda the nymphomaniac," she giggles again and smiles, "How nice of you to remember."

"Oh, yes, we thought you were marvellous in that play Cherie, in fact Sarah said…," Johnny suddenly clams up, realising that Sarah is no longer with him. There is an uneasy silence between them as they return to their table carefully carrying the two glasses of wine and two bottles of beer. He sadly recalls to himself that when he went to see that play, it was the last time he and his wife Sarah had gone out together before she had become too ill to do so again. She then went into palliative care at Redcliffe Hospital.

There is a lull in the entertainment as the guitarist packs up his equipment and the next act prepares for his spot. "What did you mean before, Johnny, when we were talking on the phone, and you said that you've had an interesting sort of day?" Danny asks, attempting to get the conversation at the table going again.

"Oh, yes," says Johnny, "Right, so did you all hear about the attempted mugging near Bracken Ridge Road this morning?"

They all nod. Johnny continues, "Well, the guy who was bashed is a sort of friend of mine," and he recounts what happened. Describing how he and Phillip were wearing similar anoraks earlier in the day while walking their identical greyhounds in the rain. After they parted Phillip had been bashed around the head by a mysterious man in a hoodie. On hearing about this attack on the six o'clock news, Johnny rushed to visit Phillip in hospital that evening. He also informed them of the strange detective who questioned Phillip about finding something, which Phillip hadn't and that the detective had not given his name or shown any ID.

"Hmm, that's interesting," says Mandy, "You don't think this guy in the hoodie might have bashed your friend Phillip by mistake, do you?"

"What do you mean?" asks Johnny, who hasn't considered this possibility.

"Well, you both must have looked very similar in the same-coloured anoraks, and you were both walking cream greyhounds. Maybe that guy in the hoodie meant to mug you instead."

"Me!!" says Johnny, incredulously.

"Yeah you!" says Mandy pointing at him, "Johnny Blakemore, the famous TV star. Maybe he thought, well, this guy must be loaded. I'll mug him."

"Or" says Danny cheekily, "Maybe he hates your acting so much, that he wanted to teach you a lesson."

Everyone laughs, but Cherie defends him by commenting, "Oh, that's not fair, you're a great actor Johnny," looking at him admiringly. Johnny smiles, but he is now thinking that maybe it is something to do with the USB that Misty found and maybe he should have mentioned it to his friend, Sergeant Murphy earlier during their phone conversation when he had the chance. He is about to tell his friends about the USB stick that Misty found when he is interrupted by an announcement from the emcee, advising that the next act is a comedian called Billy Lyre. Entering the stage is a slim, mature-looking man dressed in cargo pants, a fleecy blue and white striped shirt and looking a little tipsy who takes to the stage and proceeds to tell some awfully crude jokes about vaginas and penises. During this comedian's routine, 'Marcel and Bonnie' return from outside looking very happy and slightly intoxicated, but Johnny is convinced that their enjoyment isn't just caused by drinking alcohol.

The comedian is not going down too well with the audience, he is dying on stage. There are long silences between his crude jokes as he attempts to amuse the patrons, but no one is reacting. Occasionally a nervous laugh or giggle can be heard, which prompts him to change his tact and he begins making jokes about the audience. He infers that Sandgate people are not able to understand his sophisticated humour, saying things like, "I know you're out there; I can hear you breathing," and, "I heard Sandgate was a quiet place, but this is like working in a cemetery." This is met with even more deathly silence by the audience. The final straw regarding the comedian's crassness comes when Jenny the ticket seller emerges from the hall to be met by the comedian saying, "Oh, it looks like the stripper has arrived then." Jenny looks shocked and upset so she scurries from the room before becoming the unwitting target of any more offensive jokes. That's when the emcee decides that enough is enough and intervenes by promptly jumping onto the stage thanking a surprised-looking Billy Lyre in mid-sentence and asking for applause from the audience which ends up sounding like a couple of seals clapping their fins together. During the comedian's set and the resulting break in the entertainment, many trips have been made to the bar and to the men's room by Johnny and Danny as they have become progressively inebriated.

After one trip Danny asks Johnny, "Did you see that bald guy in a black suit, who just left?"

"Suit? What kind of person wears a suit to a place like Unplugged Cafe?" says a bemused Johnny and then answers his question. "Oh, maybe he has just come straight from work, or maybe he's a cop checking out what 'Marcel and Bonnie' might be taking tonight. Anyway, what about him?"

Ignoring the question, Danny asks with a puzzled look, "Who's Marcel and Bonnie?"

"You know?" Johnny nudges him and gives a sly look towards the strange couple who are now as high as kites.

"Oh them, yeh…." chuckles Danny, "He's a Dee Jay at the local radio station, you know Sounds of Sandgate FM?

"Really?" exclaims a surprised Johnny.

"Yeah, he goes by the name Languid Larry, because he has a laid-back, late-night Saturday show, 'Up Late with Larry' it's very popular."

"Is that right," says Johnny, trying not to laugh. Then he suddenly remembers the man at the hospital who asked Phillip all those questions. "Hey, did you say this bloke that just left was bald and he was wearing a black suit?"

"Yeh, that's right, well the lady on the door, you know, Jenny, said he reeked of cologne and after paying his five bucks, he came in and then left almost immediately. I also noticed him when he came into the room. He had a good look around the room and his stare became intently fixed on the bar for a few seconds. It looked like he had clocked someone. Then he turned around and walked straight out again. Don't you think that's a bit strange?"

"Maybe, yeah, maybe it was, but I didn't notice him. Reeked of cologne did you say? Well, where was I then, when all this was happening?"

"Oh, you were at the bar at the time, mate."

Shaking his head, "And what's your point Cheezer?"

"My point is, Blakey, he seemed to clock you at the bar and after that he promptly left."

"Not to worry, our old mate, Spud, or should I say Sergeant Mike Murphy is looking into all this. You remember the three of us at school, we were the Three Musketeers."

Danny throws a fist in the air, "Oh yes, Cheezer, Spud and Blakey, all for one and one for all."

Johnny laughs, "Good bloke Spud, he'll sort it all out, for sure."

They go back inside and resume sitting at the table just as the last act begins their set, except for Guy and Amelie that is, who knock back their red wines quite quickly saying they have seen enough for one night and hurry off bidding everyone, "A bientot."

It is now impossible to continue any sort of conversation. The community centre is buzzing as the Gypsy Blues Band proceeds to bring the house down, playing original bluesy material and the odd cover. Their act comes to a rousing finale when the band leader introduces the burlesque dancer as Gypsy Rose. She is wearing a cloak on stage and begins gyrating to the music like a belly dancer would. She then throws off her cloak and strips down to her panties, showing off her huge breasts, only just keeping her modesty by having gold stars covering her nipples.

Johnny is thinking, is this bloody legal, especially in Sandgate, maybe the bald cop in the black suit was from the vice squad and he was here to check out this act, but it's a bit of a coincidence, isn't it, if he is the same detective that spoke to Phillip at the hospital. Anyway, the audience are lapping up the show, especially 'Marcel and Bonnie,' as Johnny labelled them, who were gyrating to every move that the burlesque dancer made. Johnny is even coaxed to get up onto the dance floor during the band's performance, first by Mandy and then by Cherie. It is the first time in a long while that Johnny has let his hair down and he's really enjoying himself. He is feeling a little intoxicated now from the amount of alcohol he has consumed, and Cherie has made sure that they are dancing very close. The scent of her perfume is filling his senses, and the closeness of her body is having a satisfying sensual effect on him.

After the show, everyone gravitates outside the community hall while the four remaining members of Danny's party agree that it has been a fun night. Because they have all consumed rather a lot of alcohol, sensibility kicks in and they agree to leave their cars parked in Rainbow Street, walk home and collect them in the morning. They all live close enough to do this, so it is not a big deal. Danny and Mandy's home is in Sandgate, whilst Cherie and Johnny both live in Shorncliffe.

"You'll walk Cherie home, won't you, Johnny?" asks Mandy.

"Me? Err, oh yes of course… Err… sure, I'll do the gentlemanly thing," says Johnny thinking that he has been set up "Where is it that you live exactly, Cherie?"

"Not too far from you, as it happens Johnny, at the end of Palm Avenue," Cherie says invitingly.

"Oh… okay, err… well, that's not too far out of my way… right… uhm… let's go then." Johnny is not too sure about this.

They all say their final goodbyes, giving each other big hugs and promising to get together again very soon. Johnny and Cherie stroll along Rainbow Street, just as a green Mini Cooper passes by heading towards Sandgate, which Johnny notices again, but only because he thinks it's a nice-looking car, and he doesn't comment.

There is little conversation at first between Johnny and Cherie, but then after a while when they reach Friday Street, Cherie loops her arm around Johnny's and says to him in a childish voice, "Are you going to protect me if anyone tries to mug us, Johnny?"

"Mug us!" exclaims Johnny with a laugh, "Nobody ever gets mugged in Shorncliffe, nothing like that ever happens around here."

"You've got a short memory Johnny, what about your friend with the greyhound today?"

"Oh him, well," replies Johnny slurring his words slightly with a chuckle, "I suppose you are right, but that wasn't in Shorncliffe, was it? That was in the Deagon area, a whole different type of person over there, very deviant the people in Deagon."

"Deviant?" queries Cherie, not understanding. She has now taken off her shoes because of the high heels she was wearing, as it is much more comfortable for her to walk barefoot.

"Yeah," says Johnny, "The Deagon Deviation! Get it."

The Deagon Deviation is the name of the bypass that leads towards the bridge to Redcliffe.

"Oh yes, I get it, very funny Johnny," Cherie laughs. "At least you're funnier than that comedian was tonight." She looks at him intently, "You know? That is what I have always liked about you, Johnny."

"Well, it really wasn't that funny, Cherie."

"No, it wasn't really, was it?" agrees Cherie, teasing him.

"Anyway, Phillip wasn't technically mugged, he was just assaulted, wasn't he? Nothing was actually stolen from him."

"No, because he didn't have anything to steal, but the mugger wasn't to know that, was he Johnny?"

He doesn't argue but looks into Cherie's amazing blue eyes that now seem like translucent opals to him. "Erm… what is it that you, err… that you like about me then?" says Johnny slurring again.

"What do you mean?" replies Cherie cheekily.

"You said, just before, that there was something that you always liked about me?"

"Well, yes there is. You can make me laugh, which means you are able to make me forget all my troubles."

"Do I?" exclaims Johnny, "What kind of troubles could you possibly have then?"

"Oh, you know, loneliness, unfulfillment. I was married once you know, well I still am, I suppose."

"Oh really," said Johnny, pretending not to know about her past.

"Yeah, he's an Irish guy, his name is Declan O'Bryan, and he came out here on a working visa. I really loved him. He got me pregnant, and I had a little girl," she hesitates for a moment, "We called her Marie and afterwards we got married."

"Yes, I did know about your little girl," he says hesitantly, "She died quite young, didn't she?"

"Yes, it was a cot death, she was only a few months old." Cherie's eyes are beginning to well up with tears now and Johnny wants to put his arms around her and hug her, but he thinks better of it and decides just to pat her gently on the shoulder. "Anyway, that's all in the past. Declan became a piss pot after Marie died. He lost his job as a labourer with the local council, but afterwards he did manage to get some work on the trawlers. Suddenly, one day about three years ago, he said he was going away for a while, packed some clothes into a duffle bag and I never heard from him again. I thought he must have gone back to Cork in Ireland. However, a cousin of his, Finn, who was visiting Australia on holiday did call at the house a couple of years ago and asked where he was, so it appears that he never did return home to Ireland. Well, not then anyway as none of his relatives over there have heard from him either. He might have decided to see a bit of the world first, of course".

Johnny quietly takes in all that Cherie is telling him, and thinks it is strange that Declan would leave her, asking, "Do you think he did finally make it home to Ireland?"

"Not that I know of," replies Cherie, "I did receive a letter from his cousin Finn about a year after he visited Australia saying that Declan's Mother had died and there was still no sign of Declan."

"You could have reported it to the police, you know, after speaking with his cousin, saying that you needed to let Declan know about his mother's death?"

"Well yes, Finn reported it to the Irish police," replies Cherie, "And I went to see a Sergeant Murphy at Sandgate Police Station about a year ago, who said he would look into it for me."

"And did he?"

"Apparently," she shrugs her shoulders, "He told me later that it would be too hard to find him now as it had been a couple of years since he left me. He said the trail would now be too cold to follow and Declan could be living anywhere in the world."

They are now walking down Palm Avenue, a long and wide road lined with tall palm trees on either side. They cross the railway line at the crossing gates which are open and pass by the beautiful old Queenslander houses on either side of the road. They can hear the bats screeching in the palm trees whilst eating the seeds. The conversation now changes to Cherie's job at a local Real Estate office and how she would like to do something more challenging and about what kind of projects Johnny has lined up for the future. Johnny tells her about his upcoming audition for a pirate film and gives her a sample of his pirate accent, which cheers Cherie up. At the very end of Palm Avenue, they arrive at Cherie's place, a well-kept small wooden house that backs onto Cabbage Tree Creek. This type of house is described in Real Estate terms as a worker's cottage, with its own dock. It's the type of house that is very well sought after in the market these days.

Cherie invites Johnny in for coffee, but he declines. They've both had a skin full, and he knows where this might lead to. He feels that he isn't ready yet for a relationship and however much Cherie's body seems inviting to him and however much he longs to be with a woman again, he reluctantly leaves, but not before he politely thanks her for her company. They exchange phone numbers, and he promises to have a coffee with her in Sandgate sometime soon. Cherie seems disappointed but says, "Okay then, Johnny."

After kissing Cherie awkwardly on the cheek, Johnny decides to go the rest of the way home along Sinbad Street, which skirts Cabbage Tree Creek. This is where trawlers are moored during the day. Some mornings crew members and others set up here to sell fresh prawns and other sea foods to the public from the previous night's catch. It is all quiet now as midnight approaches. All the trawlers are now out in Moreton Bay until early morning. Johnny walks past the old Co-Op Fishing buildings, the Shorncliffe Yacht Club, the golf course and the Volunteer Marine Rescue headquarters. He is suddenly startled by a screeching fruit bat gliding out of a palm tree. As he makes his way along Allpass Parade, the tide is high up on the sea wall that was originally built by relief workers during the depression. Johnny can now feel a cold breeze on his face and his thoughts drift towards Cherie getting ready for bed, her naked body slipping between the covers all alone. He now thinks he should have stayed, had that cup of coffee and allowed for any natural developments to proceed. He feels very horny and ashamed of what Sarah might be thinking of him as she looks down on him from above. He has a vision of 'The Lady of Shalott' in her boat giving him a certain look, the same look that Sarah gave him sometimes.

Johnny can now make out the Southern Cross and Venus in the night sky. The breeze coming from Moreton Bay is getting stronger and it feels like it may rain. As he walks further along Allpass Parade he can hear the rigging flapping against the masts of the many pleasure craft in the marina. Then, as he nears his house in Jetty Street, something familiar happens to him. He hears the faint drone of a didgeridoo coming from the direction of Dinah Island. He stops and peers across Cabbage Tree Creek, whispering to himself, "Am I going mad?" Then he disregards the sound and convinces himself that he must be hearing things due to the large amount of alcohol that he's consumed that night at Unplugged Cafe.

As he passes the Shelley Inn and turns the corner into Jetty Street, he can hear a dog barking and instantly recognises it's Misty's bark. She only barks if someone knocks on the door or if the postman delivers mail in the letter box or if the electricity man reads the meter, because they need to gain access via the side of the house to do so. But no one reads meters on Friday nights do they and it couldn't be a postie either. Johnny is about to put his key in the front door when he realises that he is standing on a pile of dirt that must have spilt from a pot of ferns on his front porch.

Johnny always leaves a spare key under the plant pot, in case he loses or mislays his other one, but the spare key is still there where it should be. Johnny is thinking that someone must have used the spare key to get in and has then replaced it under the pot, possibly not realising that they have spilt dirt because it is dark. He turns his key in the lock of the door and enters cautiously.

Everything seems okay and after letting in Misty from the back yard Johnny pats her and says quietly, "Good girl, has someone been to see us then Misty?" Misty looks very agitated and goes about the house sniffing in every room. Satisfied that no one is still in the house and that nothing in the house seems to have been disturbed or taken, Johnny gives her a bowl of kibble saying, "Maybe no one was here at all Misty." He then begins to make himself a cup of tea and prepares for bed.

Later as he lays in bed, he still cannot get Cherie out of his thoughts, he remembers the sad look on her face when he gazed into her tearful blue eyes. He recalls her smooth olive skin, dark raven hair and her fabulous figure and can't get her out of his mind. He is restless and unable to go to sleep but eventually gives in to his tiredness and finally nods off.

Chapter 8

FOUL PLAY AT SEA

It is six o'clock on Friday night and the fishing trawler 'Santa Maria' is slowly chugging along the channel in Cabbage Tree Creek heading out towards Moreton Bay. Tony is at the helm looking very agitated. Manny is sitting at the rear of the trawler looking sorry for himself. Standing boldly on the bow is Ronny Carter a man in his early thirties who is looking like he is up to no good.

When the trawler is beyond Moreton Island, Tony receives a phone call and afterwards advises the other two that there is not going to be a pickup that night, but there will be tomorrow night, and as they are not fully prepared for a night of trawling they will still go through the motions as if they are, so as to avoid any unwanted scrutiny by the authorities. Manny is perfectly happy with this new arrangement and gets to work repairing any damaged nets. However, Ronny is looking very surly, constantly grumbling to himself and using disgusting expletives. He is unhappy that they will not be involved in a pickup tonight and silently blames Manny for this.

The wind has freshened during the night and the sea is rough with light rain falling in the bay, causing the trawler to rock from side to side. At around midnight, there is a low cry of pain shortly followed by a splash in the water. Tony who is at the helm of the 'Santa Maria' listening to music on the radio calls out, "What was that?" and after a short while Ronny appears saying, "It was nothing Tony, just a bull shark maybe. Everything is good... all is good.... nothing to worry yourself about."

As dawn breaks, with no trawling done at all, the 'Santa Maria' heads back towards Cabbage Tree Creek at Shorncliffe and Tony is again at the helm and wonders why he has not seen Manny for some time and when he questions Ronny, "Where's Manny?" Ronny does not answer him.

"Ronny! Where's Manny? What have you fucking done?"

Ronny has a blank expression on his face and just shrugs his shoulders saying tersely, "Maybe he fell overboard."

Tony's lips begin to quiver, he has known Manny for a long time, and he begins to sob, wondering if his own life may also be in danger. He thinks about how he got mixed up with these people in the first place, how he was talked into helping them after he got into debt and needed a financial loan, or he would lose his precious 'Santa Maria'. He pulls himself together and manages to concentrate on keeping the trawler on course and heading towards the channel at Cabbage Tree Creek and Shorncliffe.

Chapter 9

A CHANCE MEETING

Johnny is in a deep sleep. He seems to be hovering like a restless spirit above Cabbage Tree Creek. A swirling mist is gradually covering the water and, in the distance, an old-fashioned wooden craft resembling a Viking boat emerges from the mangroves on Dinah Island. The craft is heading straight towards him. In the boat is an elegant-looking lady wearing a headband and dressed in a long white gown. She is all alone and her face is very pale. She looks ill. Johnny suddenly recognises who the elegant lady is. It's Sarah, his wife who passed four years ago. She is sitting in the boat with her long auburn hair trailing down her back and she is smiling at him reassuringly. Sarah is The Lady of Shalott!

Johnny now turns over in his bed and senses in his sleepy state that it must have been a dream, but there is now a knock on the door. Johnny gets out of bed and answers it wearing only his boxers. To his surprise when he opens the front door Cherie is standing there wearing a white plastic raincoat as it's raining outside, her hair is wet, and her lips are ruby red. Not a word is spoken between them. They embrace and kiss passionately and he can taste her lipstick. He picks her up gently and carries her to his bed, undoes her buttons and puts his hands inside her raincoat. He can feel the warmth coming from her body and is now aware that she is completely naked underneath. Johnny is becoming very excited now, feeling horny as he kisses her firm breasts, then he can see that she has gold stars on her nipples. They kiss again, this time she slips her tongue into his mouth, which seems unusually long. It is still a dream.

He wakes with a start horrified to see it is not Cherie he is kissing but, "Misty! How many times have I told you not to lick me awake in the morning?" He runs to the bathroom and proceeds to wash out his mouth by putting it under the tap and then gargling it with a strong mouth freshener. After satisfying himself that he has removed any dog germs, he laughs out loud, seeing the funny side of it. He adores his pet dog.

After a long shower to clear his head from the alcohol he had consumed the night before, Johnny enjoys a strong cup of black coffee and some buttered toast for breakfast. He then takes Misty for a walk so he can retrieve his car from outside the Sandgate Community Centre, where it was left after Unplugged Cafe the night before. It is now almost nine thirty on Saturday morning and as they leave the house in Jetty Street, he again notices the dirt on the porch by the pot of ferns. "Sometimes I wish you could talk to me Misty; it was probably a cat, eh? What do you think? Yeah, probably a cat, nothing exciting ever happens around here, does it?"

"Come on girl," gently tugging Misty's leash they proceed to the end of Jetty Street, turning into Swan Street and then along Friday Street past Shorncliffe Railway Station. They pass the huge Moreton Bay Figs in Hutchinson Park and continue into Rainbow Street. As they pass Palm Avenue near the convenience store, who should Johnny see walking in the same direction, but Cherie. She looks gorgeous wearing a Sandcliffe Theatre black baseball-type cap, tight blue denim shorts, a white blouse tied in a bow at the waist and a pair of white sandals. Her navel is showing and some of her blouse buttons are undone, revealing her cleavage. Her long legs look like they could go on forever. Then his thoughts go back to his dream of being with her the night before and seeing her with gold stars covering her nipples.

"Ah, two minds with a single thought," shouts Johnny to get her attention.

"Johnny!" says Cherie cheerfully, who has turned on seeing him, "And what thought would that be?"

"Oh, I did not mean… erm… well, we are both going to collect our cars at the same time, aren't we? That is all I meant, really," says Johnny confused.

"Just teasing you Johnny," says Cherie who continues smiling and shaking her head.

Johnny laughs awkwardly and rolls his eyes as Cherie gives Misty a big hug. The dog responds by wagging her tail. "See, at least your dog loves me, don't you, Misty?" Johnny has gone blood red now.

"Do you enjoy teasing me?" says Johnny.

"Absolutely, that's what I love, I mean… what I like about you Johnny." His eyes are open wide now and his eyebrows are raised in a please explain expression.

"You do get embarrassed easily don't you, Johnny? Not all men do you know, most men just act macho when a woman says something intimate. I like your innocence ... are you a Catholic, by the way?"

"Yes, I am as a matter of fact, is it that obvious?" he sighs. Cherie nods her head and smiles. "A Catholic upbringing has a lot to answer for," sighs Johnny again. "Actually, I just consider myself a Christian these days. I don't mind what church I go to, and well, it's the same God isn't it, after all?"

"I suppose so" says Cherie, "Are you very religious then?"

"No, not really, but after losing Sarah I suppose I did find a lot of comfort by going to church regularly. It seems to be a great solace for me." Their eyes meet and a comforting smile appears on Cherie's face. He continues, "What religion are you, then?"

"Baptist, but I don't go to church all that often, just Christmas and Easter, weddings, funerals and baptisms. You know that sort of thing," she says, shrugging her shoulders.

"Baptist?" says Johnny nodding his head, "Yes Baptist is okay, I sometimes go to the old Baptist Church at the end of Flinders Parade, just near here."

"Yes, it's a lovely church, isn't it?" replies Cherie, "And in such a lovely spot by the water."

"Oh, by the way" says Johnny, "I got a bit of a scare when I returned to my place last night. I thought that someone had been there whilst I was at Unplugged Cafe."

"Thought?" says Cherie, "Aren't you sure?"

"Well, no, I'm not… I am not sure… I thought someone must have found my spare key and opened my front door, because dirt had been disturbed from the plant pot that I hide the spare key under… but it was probably just a cat or even the wind maybe as the keys were still under the pot."

"They may have just put it back afterwards."

"Yeh maybe, I suppose," agrees Johnny.

"Are you going to mention it to the police then?" enquires Cherie.

"The Police?… no… no, I don't think so… nothing appears to have been taken, they don't need me to be wasting their time, do they?"

"But are you sure that nobody was in your house last night," says Cherie pointedly.

"Look, it was most likely a cat or maybe some kids larking about… you know… I did something stupid when I was a kid… and well, this old guy just gave me a telling off and told me to wake up to myself and not to do it again. If he had handed me in to the police, I would have been in big trouble. I never forgot it and made sure that I never did anything stupid like it again."

"What was it you did, Johnny, break into someone's house?"

"No, no… it was nothing like that. Well, I… my mates said that I should steal some lollies from a corner shop counter when the owner wasn't looking. They said that they had both done it before, that it was easy."

"And what happened?"

"Well, he caught me, didn't he? As I was leaving the shop with my pockets full of lollies, he grabbed me by the scruff of my neck and made me put them all back."

"Did he know your mates had done it before?"

"That's just it, they hadn't done it before, they just said they had to get me to do it."

"Is that all! You're a big softie really, aren't you, Johnny? That is another thing I…" she pauses, "Like about you."

They have now reached their vehicles, and Johnny is about to load Misty into the back and say goodbye to Cherie, when she says, "Well, we might as well have that coffee you promised me then, what do you say?"

"What coffee?" asks Johnny looking confused.

"The coffee that you promised to have with me sometime… last night… don't you remember?"

"Last night?" Johnny has a vision of himself kissing Cherie's breast, then he remembers it was only a dream. "Oh yes, outside your house… not at my house, yes definitely at your house." Cherie looks at him strangely and he continues, "Coffee good… yes… yes okay, why don't we meet at the Town Hall Cafe in a few minutes then… yes… good… perfect!" He now has a forced embarrassed smile on his face.

Cherie says sternly, "You had better turn up," giving him a wave and driving off in her yellow Suzuki Swift while Johnny is still putting Misty into the back of his car. As he sits in the drivers' seat about to put his seat belt on, he says, "Well Misty, what do you think of Cherie? She is nice, isn't she?" Misty places her head on Johnny's shoulder and looks at him with her big brown doe like eyes, looking very cute. Johnny sighs, starts the motor saying, "Oh what am I asking you for?"

Johnny leaves his car parked behind the shops on Second Avenue and notices that Cherie is already parked there too. As he walks with Misty down the short arcade that leads to the Town Hall Café, the chimes of the Town Hall clock tell him it is now 9am. He knows the café owner is okay with dogs being there as long as they use the outside tables. Johnny secures Misty's leash to his chair and leaves her with Cherie, who is already seated. He goes inside to place their order of fruit scones with cream and jam and a pot of tea to share, rather than a coffee, after all.

As they sit there waiting for Harry, the bakery owner, to bring out their order there seems to be a procession of young women dressed in leotards passing by. Johnny and Cherie quickly work out that they are going to a newly opened fitness gym, just a couple of doors down from the Town Hall Café. The women's leotards are very figure hugging and one of the ladies in a leopard-skin leotard has one of those large bubble butts, which makes Johnny's eyes pop out and draws a disapproving look from Cherie. Another young girl on her way to the fitness gym is dressed in a lime green outfit and has those ridiculously long semipermanent fluttery eyelash extensions, which resemble garden rakes and cost an absolute fortune as they involve webbing and thatching.

Then, an Aboriginal man called Dudley Brown walks by. Dudley is a well-spoken tall, fit-looking proud Turrabul man, about fifty years old, with long greying hair and a full greying beard. He is wearing a Stetson hat and has a guitar strapped to his back. "Hi Johnny, long time no see, what have you been up to?" Before Johnny can answer Dudley has spied Cherie and says, "Oh, I can see what you have been up to, is this your girlfriend then?"

"Friend," says Johnny quickly, "Just a friend, Dudley."

"Aren't you going to introduce me to your girl fr… your friend then?" says Dudley.

"Oh, of course I am… this is Cherie, Cherie this is an old friend of mine, Dudley. Dudley helps at the Salvos in Rainbow Street and sometimes sings and plays his guitar at the Cardy Bar, just round the corner there," he points towards Bowser Parade.

"Pleased to meet you, Cherry." Cherie smiles. "You're a very attractive' lady." Cherie laughs.

Dudley pats Misty on her head.

"And what have you been up to lately, Dudley?" asks Johnny.

"Oh, nothing much really, but I did have to go to attend court recently."

"Court?" says Cherie, "Nothing serious, I hope?"

"Oh no, they just accused me of receiving stolen goods, but I soon sorted them out," says Dudley proudly.

"Oh, how did you manage to sort them out then, Dudley?" asks Johnny, thinking that he is about to be told a yarn.

"Well, I said to the Judge, how dare you accuse me of receiving stolen goods, your Honour. When you white fellas stole all our land and have been selling it and buying it again and again over the past two hundred years. You white fellas are all guilty of receiving stolen goods, don't you agree?"

"And then what happened," asks Cherie.

"The Judge said there was no case to answer and I was free to go," Dudley smiles.

They all start laughing loudly and Johnny says, "You made all that up, didn't you, Dudley?"

"Maybe," says Dudley cheekily, and then in a more serious tone, "But not the part about stealing our land."

"Fair enough,' says Johnny, noticing Cherie is trying to stop laughing.

Just then, Harry comes out with their order and Dudley bids them farewell, but not before pulling his guitar off his back and starts singing, "Cherry oh, Cherry oh baby, don't you know I'm in..."

"It's Cherie, Dudley," interrupts Johnny, "Not Cherry."

Not to be deterred, Dudley continues, "Oh, I beg your pardon," and sings, "My Cherie amour, lovely as a summer day..." and walks off chuckling to himself, but not before giving a loud wolf whistle to another slim blonde young lady, wearing a red and black leotard, who is not amused by his gesture and is now jogging along to the fitness gym as quickly as she can, her ponytail swishing from one side to the other.

Afterwards, Johnny and Cherie talk about all sorts of things whilst drinking their morning tea and even agree to meet at the Baptist church on Sunday for the 9am service, both thinking it would be a nice thing to do. Johnny also informs Cherie that after church he would like to take her to meet two old ladies, Millie and Tillie, who he sometimes visits on Sunday mornings for tea and cakes. They live at 'Cremorne,' a house in Flinders Parade in Sandgate. Cremorne used to belong to an old movie star back in the day, but the building has since been converted into units and has fallen into disrepair. They will be expecting him as he had already promised them, he'd be there on Sunday morning at about ten.

When they have finished, Cherie says, "Well… thank you for the morning tea, but I'm afraid that I must go to work now."

"Work?" enquires Johnny, sounding surprised, "On a Saturday?"

"Yes, I work at the Real Estate office in Brighton. My boss, Margie, really needs me to go in today and sort out a few things, so I will be up to speed for Monday morning. I was supposed to be there already, but Margie rang to advise that the computers were down and that they wouldn't be fixed for a couple of hours." She smiles and tells Johnny that she wishes she didn't have to go to work as she is enjoying his company.

"Computer!" exclaims Johnny, "USB! Yes, that's why someone might have been in my house last night… of course!"

"What?" says Cherie giggling.

"They must have been after the USB stick that Misty found in the wetlands yesterday."

"What USB?" asks Cherie, "You never mentioned that before."

"No, I didn't did I, sorry. I haven't told anyone about it until now. The USB that they thought Phil had... poor old Phil, I feel guilty about him being bashed now."

"What was on this USB?" says Cherie, who is now very intrigued.

"Well, that's just it, I don't know," Johnny looks confused, "It's just numbers and letters, some sort of code perhaps, I'm not sure what it means. Hey Cherie, how would you like to help me work out what this code is?"

"But Johnny. if someone broke into your place last night, isn't it possible that they have taken it back?"

"The USB? Maybe, but I saved the info, and I also wrote it down. I'm sure they wouldn't have found that."

"Okay," says Cherie, "Of course I'll try and help you figure it out," shaking her head, "But I really must go and get changed for work. Can I come round to your place afterwards, say 4pm?" Johnny nods in agreement.

"Okay, 4pm," says Johnny excitedly giving her his address and then a peck on her cheek, but it does not seem as awkward as it had been the night before.

Then they leave to retrieve their cars from the car park at the rear of the Town Hall Café. Johnny can't help admiring Cherie's legs and rear as she walks away.

After Cherie drives off, Johnny is keen to get home to check out his computer but decides not to leave straight away. He wonders if Misty would like to have a quick walk around Einbunpin Lagoon Park before leaving. It's a pleasant park with plenty of trees and lawns, a wooden pavilion big enough to house a brass band and a delightful twin-gabled timber bridge over the kidney-shaped lagoon that was once three times its size before it was filled in to create a car park. Each August an 'Einbunpin Festival' is held here, attracting hundreds of locals to sample food and crafts from the many stalls and to enjoy the live entertainment by local musicians and school bands. The Bunpin is a mythical beast that is supposed to reside here and each year someone dresses up as the creature. Johnny and Misty do a lap of the park, passing by a clump of trees covered in Ibis, also known locally as bin chickens. The lagoon contains turtles and eels, not to mention an abundance of water birds, cranes, shags, black ducks, wood ducks and waterhens for which this is their habitat. As they cross the timber bridge, the Shillam sculptures of The Cormorants, are majestically surveying the area from the centre of the lagoon. Johnny walks on past the courthouse and police station in Keogh Street on the northern side of the park and is tempted to go and tell his police friend, Sergeant Mike Murphy, about finding the USB but after deliberating for a few seconds and hearing the Town Hall clock striking 10am, he thinks better of it and decides to go back to his car and head home.

After Johnny arrives back at his house in Jetty Street, he gives Misty some dog biscuits and notices that he has a message on his landline. "Hi Johnny, Spud here, mate, that err… detective you mentioned, well mate, I've asked around all the local stations and no one can recognise him from the description you gave. I reckon Mr. Simpson must have been confused, eh, what with the knock on the head and the shock and everything. Hey, give me a call soon as you can, mate."

Johnny is now looking for the USB stick, which is not in the computer where he left it, so it is obvious that's what the intruder must have been looking for. He quickly searches on his computer, but he can't find the file that he saved either, someone must have deleted it. Then with some trepidation, he opens the "Great Expectations" novel, and thankfully the piece of paper that he wrote the code on is still there. He eagerly begins to scrutinise the letters and numbers. "What can this all be about?" he asks himself out loud.

Johnny has been staring intently at the piece of paper containing the supposed code for quite some time now. He has in front of him, various scraps of paper with jottings on it, representing some ideas or theories of his as to what this message or code, if it is a code, might be.

06/07.02:58.1.88.273365S.1532502E

It is late afternoon now and although he is not aware of the time, he wonders why Cherie hasn't arrived yet. Misty has been whimpering, so he lets her out into the backyard, believing she needs to relieve herself. He has tried all sorts of ideas and theories as to what the message could be, that's if it is a message, but he just can't work out what it is all about. What is significant about the two letters in the code, **S** and **E,** could they be South and East?

Just when he is thinking of packing it in there is a knock on the door and when he answers it, Cherie is standing there looking gorgeous again in a red and white polka dot dress, she seems slightly out of breath. "Sorry, I'm later than I said I would be," says Cherie breathlessly, "My boss needed me to go and see a prospective client and I couldn't get away any earlier."

"You look nice."

"Thank you."

"What is the time?" queries Johnny, "I can see that it's starting to get dark."

"It's Six O'clock," says Cherie embarrassed, "I'm so sorry, how did you get on with your code?"

"Six O'clock?" exclaims Johnny, "Is it that late? I've been looking at this code off and on ever since I got back from being with you. I haven't made much progress I'm afraid. Hey, no wonder Misty is getting restless, look I had better give her a feed first, then I'll get us something to eat, you must be hungry too, how about Fish and Chips from Shelley's next door, what do you say?"

"Oh, that would be great Johnny, I could smell the lovely aroma coming from the fish and chip shop when I parked the car. Yes, I'm so famished, I've only had a cup of coffee since our tea and scones at the Town Hall Cafe this morning." She sits at his desk, "Listen, why don't you let me look at this code while you feed Misty and go next door to get our dinner?"

"Okay, sounds good. Oh, Cherie," says Johnny. She looks up at him attentively. "The USB stick has gone, and I know for sure that I left it in the computer and even the file I'd created is not there anymore, it's been deleted. So, I must have had an intruder last night after all."

"Lucky you copied it onto this piece of paper then Johnny," replies Cherie, and begins to study it.

Chapter 10

SHAKESPEARE AT SHELLEYS

After Johnny opens a tin of dog food and feeds Misty, he steps outside his home and there is an eerie sight as a colony of bats fly overhead filling the sky on their way to Sandgate, something which happens every evening at dusk. He hurries next door to Shelley's fish and chip shop. When he enters, a few people are waiting for their orders, as it is a popular place on the weekend.

A good-looking teenage girl is trying to attract the attention of Jack who is serving at the counter. Jack is a lithe young man, 18 years of age, known by the shop's clientele as 'Shakespeare.' He notices her, "Yes miss?" and she replies nervously, "My Mum and Dad wanted to know if their family pack is ready yet, please? The order is number 13." After checking his unclaimed orders Jack quotes the Bard, "But soft what light through yonder window breaks? It is your family pack," he bows and presents the order to the embarrassed girl. She has gone bright red, grabs the package off him and hurries out of the door.

Jack then notices Johnny. "G'day, Mr. Blakemore, what can I get for you today?" Jack Hollis works here on the weekends; he has been in a couple of Sandcliffe Amateur Theatre Society plays and is in his first year of Drama School at QUT. Jack has known that Johnny is a professional actor for some time as his ageing Drama teacher at St Pats always spoke of him proudly as a former student. Jack has a slight build, thick black curly hair and is well known for quoting Shakespeare to the shop's customers when they receive their fish meal orders, hence the nickname.

"I'm fine Jack," says Johnny with a big smile, "Can I have two pieces of bream, a serve of calamari and a large portion of chips, thank you? And please just call me Johnny, not Mr. Blakemore."

"Strewth! Mr. Blakemore, you won't be getting many leading romantic roles if you carry on eating big meals like that," says Jack.

"Hey, don't be so cheeky," Johnny says laughing, "It's not all for me anyway."

"That'll be thirty-three dollars and fifty cents, please Mr. Blakemore."

"Don't call me Mr. Blake… oh never mind," says Johnny shaking his head and paying for the food with a credit card. Jack gives Johnny a ticket with the number 17 on it.

As Johnny turns away from the counter to wait for his order, he notices some of the other customers smiling at him. He is well known in the neighbourhood as the actor who lives in Jetty Street. He pretends not to notice their stares and busies himself by looking at the old photos of bygone days in frames on the wall of Shelleys. The collection includes a photo of his own house that was taken in the 19th Century. Johnny has of course perused these many times previously. The building had once been a hospital and when he was a high school student he had met and talked to locals who had been born there. This had been for a school project, but those people would have all passed away by now. After being a hospital, the building was Rouse's Oyster Saloon and now Shelley's Fish and Chips.

Johnny, along with the other customers are being kept amused by Jack, who presents their required orders as if he is doing a Shakespearean play as follows:

"Number 14! Whiting and Chips and a serve of Calamari. Calamari, calamari my kingdom for a Calamari, number 14."

"Number 15! Snapper and Chips…. Alas, poor Snapper, I knew him well, number 15, a fellow of infinite jest, of most excellent fancy."

"Number 16! Is this a Cod and Chips for two I see before me, number 16?"

When Jack calls out "number 17," Johnny quickly raises his hand saying, "Here!" to prevent any more of Jack's verse and approaches the counter handing him his ticket saying, "How's the Drama course going at Uni, Jack?"

Then Jack goes back into his performance mode, "If you prick me do I not bleed… if you tickle me do I not laugh… and if you poison me do I not die," while holding the parcel of food in his right hand and the back of his left hand against his forehead in a mock pose.

Johnny takes his order saying, "Sounds like it's going very well then Jack, or should I say Shylock… see you next time."

"Thanks, see you Mr… er… Johnny," Jack is now giving a low theatrical bow as Johnny leaves the building, fish and chips in hand.

Chapter 11

LETTERS AND NUMBERS

Johnny returns to the house with the parcel of seafood and chips, which he places on the kitchen table. He opens a bottle of Chardonnay that was being chilled in the fridge and pours out two glasses. "I hope this is alright. You can have a cup of tea or coffee if you would prefer."

"No, no," says Cherie cheerfully, "This is wonderful."

They eat their food whilst discussing the code, Johnny explains his theory that S and E could mean South and East. He also mentions the phone call from Sergeant Murphy and the fact that he hasn't mentioned the USB or the code to him yet.

"Well," she says, after pondering over the code a little longer, "It's probably some sort of map reference for this area, isn't it."

"No, not a map reference exactly," says Johnny, because this has prompted him to have a new idea. "I know what it is, it's a nautical reference, something to do with longitude and latitude, what do you reckon?"

"Oh yes," agrees Cherie "It is nautical isn't it, let's have another look." She scrutinises the code again. "Look, the last bit is **273365S** that could be 27.3365 degrees South, so the other bit **1532502E** is probably 153.2502 degrees East." They look at each other excitedly, being drawn into each other's eyes.

"Brilliant," says Johnny, "So which one's Latitude and which one's Longitude?"

"Google it!!" they say together laughing.

Cherie looks at her iPad and quickly works out that it is Latitude 27.3365 South and Longitude 153.2502 East, "It's near Mud Island in Moreton Bay," exclaims Cherie.

"Mud Island?" questions Johnny, "What could they possibly be getting up to over there?" Mud Island is situated in Moreton Bay, near the Port of Brisbane, a popular fishing area for canoeists.

"Some sort of illegal fishing?" suggests Cherie, "I have a kayak, maybe we could paddle out there sometime and see if we can find anything," seeing the worried look on Johnny's face she begins to smile "If you are game that is?"

"Are you serious?" says an unbelieving Johnny, "How far away is Mud Island anyway?"

"Only about ten kilometres," she says matter of factually. "You're fit enough for that aren't you? So shall we keep working on this code?" she asks expectantly.

"You wouldn't mind staying for a bit longer then, Cherie?" he says hesitantly.

"I'll stay all night if you want me to," is her bold reply.

Johnny looks into her big blue eyes and thinks how gorgeous she is. "Hmm, I… I don't think that would be a good idea, Cherie. It's just too soon for me… you know… I'm sorry."

"Oh, I see… don't you fancy me then?" says Cherie with a quiver in her voice.

"Oh yes, of course I do," sighs Johnny "Very much so, it would be the easiest thing in the world for me to pick you up and carry you into my bedroom and make love to you."

"So why don't you then?" queries Cherie, getting as close to him as she can and putting her hands on his chest.

He kisses her tenderly on both cheeks and looks into her eyes, "I really like you Cherie, we seem to be getting on pretty good together, don't we? We have a similar sense of humour, and I think that in time we could be become close friends, well maybe more than friends, but I'm just not ready at this moment in time, I'm sorry."

"Well Johnny," says Cherie sniffling, her blue eyes filling up with tears, "I think we both need to have someone, don't you? I'm not some easy lay you know; I don't just jump into bed with anyone."

"Oh, please don't think that Cherie, I never thought for a minute that you were an..." says Johnny feeling guilty. They embrace and kiss like a couple of teenagers on their first date. Johnny hasn't felt like this for a long time.

She sniffles again and regains her composure, "So Johnny, when you are ready, I'm still going be there for you."

After being unable to work out what the rest of the code might be, and as the time is 10pm, Johnny suggests that Cherie should go home. She seems very tired from working most of the day and they agree on a time to meet the next day outside the old Baptist Church for the 9am service as they had planned whilst at the Town Hall Café that morning. Then after the service Johnny wants to surprise Millie and Tillie, the Smith Twins at 'Cremorne,' by taking Cherie to visit them with him for morning tea. Johnny walks Cherie to her car where they have a long lingering kiss, and he watches her drive away towards the western end of Jetty Street and out of sight. Shelleys is closed now, and all is quiet in the area, except for the occasional squealing of a fruit bat and the low chugging sound of a trawler as it heads out into Moreton Bay.

After Johnny has washed up and cleared everything away, he gets changed for bed. For a while he ponders the piece of paper containing the code and the remaining part of it that they couldn't work out **06/07.02:58.1.88** then puts the paper on his bedside table, sets his alarm for 7:30am, so he will have ample time to get ready for church the next morning and turns out the lights and gratefully falls into bed.

Chapter 12

CHERIE REFLECTS

Cherie arrives home a bit teary and upset that Johnny didn't want her to stay, but she is hopeful that this could be the start of something good, something that will be worthwhile for them both. They need each other, she knows it, it's just that Johnny doesn't know it yet. She is convinced he will come around eventually and realise that he can't live without her. Cherie also reflects on her life; she has had some tragedies over the years that have made her into a strong woman. She was born in the small town of Cowaramup, near Margaret River in West Australia. When she was only twelve years old her parents were killed when their car was involved in a head-on crash with a truck which Cherie miraculously survived almost without a scratch. After that, she was raised by her grandparents in Perth who have now passed on. She moved to Brisbane when she was an adult and eventually settled in Shorncliffe making a good life for herself in the real estate industry. When she hooked up with Declan, he was a bit of a wild one, but she managed to calm him down and life was good at first. However, that all changed after the death of their daughter, Marie. She was the best thing that came out of their marriage, it made Declan grow up and be a man and to be a father. He was a good father, he loved Marie, and he worked hard to provide for his family. Things were looking good, he was saving up money, because he wanted to take Cherie and Marie back to Ireland for a holiday to visit his mother and he would have been so proud to show off his new wife and daughter to his whole family. But after Marie died, he turned back to the drink, he was always at the Seaview Hotel with his mates and the marriage was doomed to fail. Cherie is very tired now and slips between the sheets on her bed, she is lying on her back looking up at the ceiling and wishing that she was looking up at Johnny and they were making love. Eventually, she gives in to her tiredness and slowly drifts off to sleep.

Chapter 13

A TRIP TO MUD ISLAND

Johnny hasn't been asleep for long when he senses that he is floating above Cabbage Tree Creek again, there is a swirling thick mist, and he sees an old-fashioned boat in the distance emerging from the mangroves on Dinah Island and it's heading directly towards him. In the boat sits an elegant lady wearing a headband and dressed in a long white dress, she is alone, her face is very pale, and she looks ill. It's Johnny's wife Sarah again, but this time she is not smiling at him, she is looking very concerned and wagging a warning finger at him.

He wakes with a start, trying to make some sense of the dream that he's just had and then he looks at his illuminated digital alarm clock in the dark, the time is 10:46.

"That's it!" he says out loud, "That's it, it's the time." He turns on the light and looks at his piece of paper with the code, "So **02:58** is the time, therefore **06/07** is the day, tomorrow morning!" What was left, **1.88**, but he has no idea what that means.

He immediately phones Cherie who takes a while to answer her mobile. "Cherie, thank god you answered, I've worked it out, I've worked it out," he says excitedly. "It's tomorrow 06/07, 6th July is tomorrow at 2:58 in the morning at Mud Island, no wonder they wanted the USB back so quickly, I've no idea what **1.88** means though."

"Ah, I think I do Johnny," she says interrupting him proudly, then Cherie urges him to put on some warm clothes and get over to her place as quickly as possible.

Johnny excitedly pulls on a pair of jeans, a T-shirt and jumper, and a pair of trainers, puts Misty on the back porch and drives to Cherie's place as fast as he can. When he arrives in Palm Avenue, she is already dressed in an anorak, brown cord jeans and is wearing a snugly fitting Sandcliffe Amateur Theatre Society cap, with the letters S.A.T.S. She is also triumphantly holding up a July copy of the Sandgate Guide, a free publication for what's on in the area and has it opened at the page that gives the July Tide Chart and is pointing at Sunday 6th July High Tide of 1.88 metres at 02:58am.

"Brilliant!" exclaims Johnny, "What do we now?"

"Shush Johnny," she puts her finger to her lips, "Keep your voice down, we don't want to upset the neighbours," pleads Cherie in a low voice, and they hug each other joyously but quietly.

"So, what happens now?" whispers Johnny, looking intently into her beautiful blue eyes.

"Are you up for a paddle out to Mud Island tonight then?" replies Cherie, giggling at the worrying expression appearing on his face.

"I will if you will," he nervously replies.

Cherie leads Johnny to the rear of her property where there is a kayak of the snap variety, it is in two pieces and snaps together in the centre to make a one-person kayak, but when you insert a third centrepiece, it then becomes a two-person kayak. Johnny seems concerned that the craft will stay together out on the bay if it starts to get rough, but she assures him that it is quite sea-worthy. Cherie has now produced the paddles and the yellow life preservers, which she tells him they must both wear, she also finds Johnny some old boat shoes, that must have belonged to her husband Declan and puts a compass in her pocket, just in case they get disorientated during their adventure. Then they quietly place the kayak onto Cabbage Tree Creek under some mangrove trees by a dock at the rear of her house, Johnny is at the front and Cherie is behind him, and they start paddling, slowly at first along Cabbage Tree Creek until they are out into Moreton Bay, which fortunately is quite calm at the present. Johnny takes a while to get into a rhythm, but as he gains more confidence with the kayak being safe and not going to sink, they eventually manage to paddle along in unison swapping sides occasionally when Cherie calls out, "Change." It is now nearly midnight, so they need to get a move on if they are to arrive at Mud Island before 2:58 am, as it is some way off.

The moon is almost full as they paddle across Moreton Bay. Johnny is so grateful that the sea is calm, but he can't believe that he is paddling in a kayak at midnight into the middle of Moreton Bay in the middle of Winter. He notices that wherever the position of the kayak is, the reflection of the moon on the water always seems to reflect a path of light directly towards them, but he does know this is only an optical illusion. He is also a tad concerned that they might be mowed down by a trawler on the bay, or even a large ship leaving or entering the Port of Brisbane, but Cherie who has been a kayaker since she was very young, assures him that everything will be alright and if they should see a vessel coming close to them, she will ensure they will be seen by her turning on a battery operated light that she has at the rear of the kayak.

"This is exciting," says Cherie, "I've never been out on the bay this late at night before."

"Oh, haven't you, that is so very reassuring," says Johnny sarcastically.

"Oh now, come on Johnny, where is your sense of adventure? Just imagine you are the hero in one of your films and you are going to save the whole world."

"I don't feel much like a hero at the moment," he says. "You are so wrong if you think I'm like some of the macho characters I've portrayed on screen, I'm nothing like that really and I would hate for anything bad to happen to you after I've dragged you into this mysterious caper."

"That's very sweet of you Johnny, but we'll be just fine, and anyway, I am also very curious as to what this could all be about, you know?"

Johnny suddenly has a thought, if the USB stick has been retrieved by the bald man in the black suit, then he must know the rendezvous' details as well, so won't he or somebody else be out here for whatever reason this is all about. He decides not to mention this to Cherie however, as it may alarm her, but then he thinks perhaps it won't, as nothing seems to faze her at all, she seems to be right in her element and relishing the whole experience so far. "Mmm… maybe we should have called the police, when we found out about these rendezvous details and just let them deal with it instead," he says thinking out loud and looking back at her. Cherie replies, "But we're here now, aren't we Johnny, so let's just go with the flow, okay?"

Go with the flow, indeed, thinks Johnny as he battles against the breeze, which is getting stronger, causing ripples to appear on the water. They continue paddling across Moreton Bay getting ever closer to the uninhabited Mud Island. Cherie is an experienced kayaker and because she is a member of the Shorncliffe Kayaking Club, has been to Mud Island many times before, but always during daylight hours and always with a group of paddlers. At low tide the island is covered in mud, hence its name, but it also has a forest of mangroves. When it is high tide the sea water floods over the island allowing kayakers to paddle and explore the different kinds of life that make their home on it. It's been reported that in the nineteenth century, ships would be quarantined out here and burials for the dead happened on this island.

"You are doing really well Johnny; you will have to become a member of the kayaking club."

"Maybe I will," replies Johnny, who seems to be becoming more competent in kayaking now.

They paddle on, but keep their silence, not just because they may be heard, but to conserve their energy as it is a long paddle out to Mud Island. After what seems to Johnny to be a lifetime, the sea breeze has strengthened further and Johnny whispers after checking his watch, "It is 1:55 now, how much further is it?"

"Not too much further," replies Cherie, "We can take our time now, we'll arrive in plenty of time to see what's going on, that is, if anything is going on."

When they reach the south tip of Mud Island, Johnny can see that is exactly what it is, a low-level island of mud with mangrove trees. To Johnny it doesn't seem like an island at all, just a lot of mangroves sticking up out of the sea and he cannot imagine anything but a kayak being able to navigate this area, which is full of seagrass. The island has been created by all the silt that flows down the Brisbane River out into Moreton Bay and gets deposited here. From here they can see the Port of Brisbane which is not too far away. This is where cargo ships and tankers arrive at the head of the river to unload. The huge cranes or the skeletal giraffes as Johnny likes to imagine them can now be seen quite clearly, as they are all lit up throughout the night.

Suddenly Johnny begins to gag as he is overcome by a stench of rotting fish, "My god Cherie, what is that, it smells like we are in a sewer?"

Cherie replies nonchalantly, "Oh that... sometimes trawlers dump their spoiled fish here after a night's catch before returning to Cabbage Tree Creek."

"How did you find out about that?" says Johnny putting his arm across his mouth in a futile attempt to stop inhaling the foul smell.

Cherie seems slightly embarrassed, "Oh, I think some trawler guy told me about it. And I probably should warn you that because of the rotting fish being dumped here, it does attract quite a lot of bull sharks to the area." Johnny's mouth opens wide, but he closes it again quickly due to the rotting odour. Cherie continues, "A few years ago a kayaker had a very lucky escape out here when a shark bit a piece out of his kayak causing it to begin sinking. Fortunately, he had his mobile phone with him, and he managed to make a triple-zero call which enabled the water police to track his location and rescue him."

Johnny goes pale, he knows that they don't have their mobile phones with them, having decided to leave them at Cherie's place, "Well maybe it would have been a good idea if you could have told me all about this before we set off on our trip? But we don't want any water police out here do we, well not yet anyway?"

Before Cherie can answer him, there's a sudden splash in the water, catching them both by surprise and Johnny struggles to keep his paddle flat on the water as the kayak wobbles. "Is that a shark?" he enquires with some trepidation. "No," she replies firmly, "It's probably just a dugong feeding on the sea grass." He is about to say something else but is distracted by the increasingly loud roar of a ship's engines.

They both see a cargo ship heading towards the port getting closer and closer to them, as the seconds tick nearer to 2:58am. Johnny is worried about their safety and Cherie assures him that the ship will not come too close to Mud Island, as it is too shallow, so they are in no danger, but they must be wary of the wake that the ship causes. Almost right at the time of 2:58 the cargo ship passes close by them, and they hear a large splash in the sea, as if something has been dropped from the vessel. As the ship passes them there's an enormous din coming from the engines and propellers. Johnny is worried they might capsize from the swell that the ship is causing, or be drawn into the ship's propellers, but Cherie shows him again how to steady the kayak by putting their paddles flat on the sea's surface, to avoid them taking on any water. After the cargo ship has passed, they notice a large black plastic package floating in the water not too far away from them, it has been highlighted by light created by the path of the moon shining on the water and they eagerly paddle towards the black plastic object glinting in the moonlight, keen to see what it might be.

When they draw alongside the large package, Johnny says in a low voice, "So this is what it's all about then?" Cherie nods, she now has a rope in her hand that is tied to the rear of the kayak and instructs Johnny to secure the rope to the plastic package, while she ensures that the kayak remains stable by again laying her paddle flat and close to the water.

After he's done as Cherie has requested, she says, "Okay, let's get out of here before someone comes."

Johnny looks surprised, "So you have worked out that as they found my USB, someone else would be here as well?"

Cherie replies in a serious tone, "Of course I did, but apart from them, we had better watch out for the coastguard or they might think that we are part of this conspiracy too, not to mention what the smugglers might do to us if they find out we've nicked their contraband."

"What!" exclaims Johnny.

"Oh Johnny, just think of all this as a great experience and good practice for you should you land that Pirate part you told me about on Friday night," replies Cherie in a lighter tone.

They can now hear the chugging sound of a smaller vessel and make out the shape of a trawler in the distance slowly moving towards them.

"Coastguard… smugglers? Oh, right" says Johnny urgently, "Okay let's get out of here."

"Okay, says Cherie, but first take off your life preserver, it's yellow, so they will spot us for sure if we are wearing them." They both take off their preservers, stow them in the kayak and begin to paddle in a westerly direction back towards Shorncliffe.

It is taking them a lot longer to return to Shorncliffe than it had to get to Mud Island, for one thing the breeze has stiffened, the sea is much rougher, and it is spitting with rain. Apart from that, they are dragging a large plastic package behind them. The bag seems to float easily enough on the water as if there is some kind of floatation device inside it, but to Johnny it seems like they are hardly moving at all at times and his arms are aching from the paddling. At the same time, he does admire how well Cherie is coping, she's a real trooper. They glance behind them occasionally because in the moonlight they can see a trawler manoeuvring around the bay in a sort of zig-zag pattern. In turn, they hope that the crew of the trawler can't spot them in the moonlight as they paddle furiously back towards Shorncliffe. Absolutely spent and with dawn breaking they finally arrive just south of the estuary into Cabbage Tree Creek and agree to shelter out of sight, just inside the edge of the mangrove trees on the easterly edge of Dinah Island. They are aware that they might attract a lot of attention by towing a black plastic bag down the channel. Breathing very heavily, they sit on the kayak cuddling up to each other, side by side attempting to keep warm. Johnny can hear a sound coming from deep inside Dinah Island's mangrove forest, "Can you hear a didgeridoo, Cherie?" and she wearily replies, "Sounds like an angry dog to me."

It is starting to get lighter now and the tide is going out, so to remain unnoticed they need to stay out of sight on the edge of Dinah Island. From their position they can see Baxter's Jetty at the head of Cabbage Tree Creek and out in Moreton Bay a trawler is heading towards Shorncliffe after its night out. They sense this might be the same vessel they foiled earlier near Mud Island, the one that should have picked up the contraband from the cargo ship. And as dawn is breaking the trawler may have decided to return to their mooring in Sinbad Street. Our exhausted couple wait out of sight trying to keep warm by continuing to cuddle each other as they are both very damp and chilled to the bone. When there is no longer any sight of the trawler, they are certain has been looking for them and the contraband, they come to a decision to hide the kayak, paddles, preservers and the big plastic package in the mangroves on Dinah Island. This seems to be all they can do for now as it is low tide and impossible for them to paddle back until there is a high tide again. They conceal everything high enough up in a pandanus tree, about 10 metres in from the edge of the mangroves, ensuring that nothing will be seen from out to sea, or from the Shorncliffe foreshore or affected by the next high tide. After that, they nonchalantly walk arm in arm like any loving couple along the stretch of sand back towards Shorncliffe fully intending to tell the police of their night adventure when they can get to their mobile phones, which they have left at Cherie's place.

Chapter 14

AN UNEXPECTED
TURN OF EVENTS

It is the early hours of Sunday morning on the 6th of July and the 'Santa Maria' trawler is once again out in Moreton Bay, but the crew of Tony Pesaro and Ronny Carter are not interested in fishing tonight, they are after a much more profitable cargo. The 'Santa Maria' hangs around the southern end of Moreton Island waiting for a signal from a ship that is about to enter the Port of Brisbane. A flashing signal can be seen coming from a cargo ship passing close to Mud Island before it enters the Brisbane River. Reacting to this the trawler begins heading towards Mud Island. They have done this type of pick-up many times before and it has become second nature to them, but they don't know that they have been beaten to the contraband. When they arrive at the spot near Mud Island, they soon realise that this is not how the routine normally works, because they are finding it difficult to locate the plastic bag, they can't see it anywhere, it is not where it should be. Ronny says, "Where the fuck is it! It must have sunk!" Tony replies, "It can't have sunk Ronny, it's got foam inside to keep it afloat." Thinking that the plastic package may have drifted towards the mainland, due to the increasing strength of the wind coming in from the east the trawler starts making zig-zag patterns to try to locate and retrieve the contraband. But after a frustrating few hours and the fact that dawn is beginning to break, Tony decides to head back to Cabbage Tree Creek and to face the consequences, whatever they may be.

Chapter 15

BACK ON DRY LAND

Johnny and Cherie are now walking towards Shorncliffe along the sand, which is now exposed because of the low tide. They are picking their way around the pools of water left by the tide going out. They make sure that they don't step into the small holes in the sand that have been left by feeding stingrays at low tide. Also avoiding the armies of blue soldier crabs that are darting around as they approach them, looking cute and vulnerable as they bury themselves in the wet sand. A squadron of cormorants is enjoying an eating frenzy on a school of small fish out to sea. Johnny spies P1 and P2 in their usual spot on this side of Cabbage Tree Creek and tells Cherie about how he and his daughter Sophie chose the names of the proud pelicans when she was a little girl. Cherie can only raise a weak smile, but she is holding onto him a little bit tighter now. They swim across the channel opposite Baxter's Jetty and are both dripping wet as they emerge from the water walking up the slipway for small boats. As they head towards Johnny's place in Jetty Street, they receive some strange looks from the people fishing off the Jetty and from joggers and dog walkers in Allpass Parade. The time is 8.00am when they enter Johnny's home in Jetty Street and Misty is frantically waiting to greet them. Whilst Cherie is taking a shower, Johnny notices that he has a message on his landline and presses play. "Hi Johnny, Sergeant Murphy here again, I mean Mike… we found the owner of the blue commodore, seems it was just a couple of teenagers making out… errr… give me a call mate, as soon as you can, will you?"

When Cherie emerges from the shower wearing only a Maroon's State of Origin beach towel, Johnny shows her some of his daughter's clothes that are still in her wardrobe, suggesting she might like to change into something clean and dry as they should fit okay because of her similar clothes size to Sophie. Cherie chooses some cream capri slacks and an AC/DC Tee shirt, she still has her own boat shoes to wear, and she transfers the compass from her wet clothes to her borrowed slacks pocket. After Johnny finishes showering, he puts on a pair of cargo shorts and a pale blue polo shirt. Cherie has put her wet clothes into a small plastic bag that Johnny has provided, and they head off to her home on foot via Allpass Parade and Sinbad Way. Johnny needs to collect his car, which he parked outside Cherie's place the night before and they both need to collect their mobile phones and Johnny's car keys which had been left at Cherie's house, as they didn't want to lose them during their night escapade out on Moreton Bay. They intend to call the police as soon as they arrive at her house, but first they need to eat as they are both famished, and Cherie has promised Johnny a full Aussie breakfast.

The shortest way to Cherie's house is past the moored white, blue and yellow trawlers in Sinbad Way. After their nights trawling, freshly cooked prawns are being sold to the public alongside Cabbage Tree Creek. As they pass by, they notice a trawler called the 'Santa Maria' owned by a Spaniard, Tony Pesaro standing next to a white van that is parked in front of his trawler. Cherie knows him quite well, as she has regularly purchased prawns from him in the past, her house only being 150 metres away from his dock. Tony and Cherie wave to each other as she passes, and Cherie comments, "Not selling any prawns today, Tony?"

"Ola Cherie, no, no," he replies in a thick Spanish accent, "Not a good night, last night" and then Tony takes his mobile phone out of his pocket and begins to make a call.

There is also a heavily built man in his thirties busying himself on the deck of the Santa Maria, who Cherie doesn't recognise. "Where's Manny?" Cherie asks Tony.

"Not well, had to get someone else to help last night" indicating Ronny, who is now looking at them in a surly manner with his arms folded.

"Friend of yours?" enquires Johnny to Cherie in a low voice.

"Not really, just buy prawns off him sometimes," says Cherie.

"Oh, so I guess he might be the same trawler guy who told you about the fish dumping and the bull sharks?" says Johnny inquisitively.

Cherie looks very embarrassed and doesn't answer him.

They carry on walking past another trawler selling all different types of prawns, and a well-tanned woman standing at a counter on the shore asks them, "Do you want some cooked prawns my lovelies? The boys had a very good night out on the bay last night, so we can give you a good discount, only fifteen dollars a kilo for Tiger prawns." Cherie thinks to herself that this is an excellent price as they usually charge twenty dollars a kilo, but she just smiles back at the woman who is shrugging her shoulders as they carry on walking.

When they've almost arrived at Cherie's house, a green Mini Cooper flashes past them and screeches to a halt outside and inside the car is a bald man wearing a black suit, who then raises his mobile phone to his ear. Johnny ushers Cherie to the rear of her property, and they creep along the creek's edge under the same mangrove trees from where they launched her kayak the night before. He tells her that he's sure the man in the Mini Cooper is the same one that Danny had seen acting suspiciously at 'Unplugged Café' on Friday night, a bald man in a black suit. He's also sure it's the same car that he has noticed driving around the vicinity in the past couple of days. Cherie also notices that Tony Pesaro is now standing in the road by his trawler looking towards them and he is holding his mobile to his ear and is frantically shouting into it. They baulk at going into her house, as they feel in danger of being trapped in there. Knowing they urgently need to get away, even if they can't retrieve their mobiles or Johnny's car keys from the house. Cherie's car is in the drive, and fortunately it is not locked, and she has a spare set of car keys under the driver's seat. They get into the car; Cherie drops her bag of wet clothes into the back seat, saying, "I don't understand, how do they know it was us who was out on the bay?"

As they drive off out onto the road at full speed straight down Palm Avenue Johnny replies, "Well they knew I had the USB didn't they, so they must have worked out that we deciphered the code." The Mini is soon hot in pursuit, but still a good fifty metres behind. The Suzuki arrives at the railway crossing near the top of Palm Avenue and the crossing lights are beginning to flash, Cherie puts her foot to the floor and speeds across the crossing just as the barrier is coming down barely missing them. The Mini screeches to a halt and swerves slightly to the side to avoid hitting the barrier. A few moments later the train passes on its way to Shorncliffe, giving Johnny and Cherie a couple of minutes head start.

Cherie, is now driving towards Rainbow Street and is confused, saying, "I don't quite understand, Johnny, why are we trying to get away from this detective, don't we want to tell the police all about this?"

"Yes Cherie, but the proper police," replies Johnny "We don't know if he is a real detective or not do we? And even if he is, he could be a bent cop who is mixed up in all of this."

"Did you notice the trawlerman, Tony Pesaro?" asks Cherie, her heart pumping, "I thought he was acting rather strange, I've known him for a number of years, and he seems like such a nice man, he even asked me out on a date."

"And did you go out with him?" asks Johnny.

"Yes, I did, but only a couple of times, he always smelt of fish." Cherie is now holding her nose with her thumb and finger of her right hand whilst taking a sharp left turn into Rainbow Street and heading towards Sandgate Village. "You know, I'm sure Tony tipped off the driver of that mini by letting him know that we were heading back to my house and wasn't it strange that he said they'd had a bad night trawling, and the woman selling prawns for the other trawler claimed it was an excellent night."

"I didn't like the look of your friend Tony's crew mate" says Johnny, "Wouldn't like to meet him in a dark alley at night."

"Tony's not really a friend," retorts Cherie.

"Well used to be a friend then," adds Johnny. "The Santa Maria must have been the trawler that we thought was looking for us last night, well they weren't out there fishing, were they? So, what do we do now?" he thinks for a moment, "What's the time?" looks at his watch, "8:55am."

They instinctively look at each other, both having a simultaneous lightbulb moment and shout in unison, "Church!" and after circling the Anzac War Memorial and past the Sandgate Town Hall, with the clock showing the time as 8:58am, Cherie drives on to the old Baptist Church in Cliff Street. They are both sure that they should be safe in a church amid a flock of parishioners, well for a while at least.

Chapter 16

SANCTUARY

Cherie parks her car in Cliff Street, and they walk at a fast pace towards the corner with Flinders Parade and the entrance of the magnificent old wooden Baptist Church, with its elegant spire and simple but beautiful rose windows. The church had its first congregation on Christmas Eve 1887 and has been used by various bodies in the community ever since. They are just looking to spend a little time here to get some breathing space, so they can think things through, work out what they are going to do next.

"Well, we did say we'd meet here this morning, so here we are," says Johnny as they enter the church's open door. Cherie just nods her head agreeing with him, such a lot has happened since yesterday when they had scones and tea at the Town Hall Café, where they agreed to meet at this church the next day.

They collect various leaflets and bulletins from the smiling ushers and greeters at the front entrance of the church, and after finding a row of empty pews on the right side of the aisle about halfway along they sit down. A man walks up to them and introduces himself as Chris and says to Cherie, "Acca-Dacca! Nice Tee shirt."

"Thanks," says Cherie, looking down at her Tee shirt and rolling her eyes at Johnny.

There is a large simple wooden cross on the right side of the stage which does not resemble a traditional altar, there are four people on the stage, a thick set young man wearing a checked flannel shirt with a guitar, a saxophonist with a long beard, who looks like Ned Kelly, an attractive dark haired lady on keyboards and a heavily pregnant young woman wearing a long tight figure hugging orange and white hooped dress who is holding a microphone. The Baptists do not have a set liturgy, their services are pretty much an ad hoc event. Just then the guitarist welcomes everyone and announces that they will start with "Bless the Lord, Oh My Soul," the words are projected onto a large screen, and they begin to sing as the front doors of the church are closed by a warden:

"Bless the Lord, Oh my soul, Oh my soul worship his holy name "

Suddenly there is a loud squeal from a vehicle's tyres outside the church, causing all the congregation's heads to turn their attention towards the open doors on the left-hand side of the church. The noise has been made by a green Mini Cooper coming to a sudden halt. Johnny and Cherie glance at each other, both knowing that the bald guy must have spotted Cherie's car parked outside in Cliff Street.

"Didn't take him long to find us, did it?" whispers Cherie.

There are about 50 people in the church, the door on the right side is slightly open and although they are tempted to leave by that exit straight away, they feel much safer in the church than being outside, well for the time being anyway. When the congregation finish singing the hymn, Johnny and Cherie can hear the creak of the front door opening behind them and glancing behind they both see the bald man in a black suit, who is now wearing sunglasses entering the church. He reluctantly receives a leaflet from an elderly usher and then peruses the parishioners and quickly spots where the runaways are seated.

Another song is introduced by the heavily pregnant singer, "I will run to you."

She has a beautiful voice, which Johnny and Cherie can only admire, but when she comes to the part of the song:

"And I will run to you, to your words of truth, not by might, not by power, but to the spirit of god."

Johnny can feel the bald man's eyes burning into the back of his head, he holds Cherie's hand to reassure her as she now seems quite nervous, and although it wasn't this church, he can't help being reminded of when he married Sarah and then being at her funeral, and he is now imagining her coffin before the altar. He does receive some solace by holding Cherie's hand and remembers when Sarah was sick with cancer, and she told him that it would be alright for him to find someone else after she had gone.

After the song, Chris, who turns out to be the pastor for the day, asks everyone to make themselves known to each other. This is when the parishioners turn and shake hands with people around them and they say things like "Hi, I'm Tom, God be with you, Peace be with you."

Johnny and Cherie do likewise "Hi I'm Johnny," "Hi I'm Cherie." Whilst this is going on they can see the embarrassed bald man at the rear of the church, he does not seem to know about this tradition and does not want to shake anyone's hand, let alone tell them who he is, but a couple of smiling parishioners insist that he does so.

There is no communion today, but another song is played during the offering, "Glorious Ruins" that is when a collection is made around the church and a couple of ushers go from aisle to aisle with a brown cotton bag. Johnny's wallet is also at Cherie's place, so he pretends to put his hand in his pocket and put some money in the bag, Cherie watches the usher as he moves back along the aisles. The saxophonist comes into his own now, his dulcet tones filling every corner of the church. Cherie notices that the usher is now facing the bald man and is blocking his view of them as he struggles to get his wallet out of his inside suit pocket to add to the offering. Cherie catches sight of a gun holster inside his suit jacket. She tugs at Johnny's arm, and they quickly head out the door that has been left slightly open on the right-hand side of the church. Slipping through the opening they are now outside on the footpath and walk briskly down Flinders Parade heading north, there is no sign of the bald man following them yet.

Chapter 17

MORNING TEA WITH THE SMITH SISTERS

"Had to get us out of there Johnny, I'm sure he's got a gun in a holster," she pats the left side of her chest. "Didn't want anyone in the church to get hurt."

"At least we didn't have to listen to the sermon," says Johnny grinning, but then realising what she has just said, becomes more serious, "A gun! Are you sure?"

Sounding a little worried she asks, "So what do we do now?"

"Well," Johnny hesitates for a moment, "Do you remember yesterday when I said that I would introduce you to the Smith sisters? Well, they just happen to live a couple of hundred metres from here, down Flinders Parade."

"So, what is the plan?" asks Cherie positively.

"Plan?" says Johnny sheepishly, "No, I don't have any plan at the moment, let's just get away, okay?"

"Well, we had better come up with a plan quickly Johnny," says Cherie, "Or I am going to have to call the police as soon as we get to your friend's place."

They start walking along the pavement in front of the houses in Flinders Parade and notice the Pop-Up Artists on the water-front. Sandgate Artists Society, or SasArt as they are known, meets here on the first Sunday of every month. One of their members, Cody Black spots them across the street and shouts out, "Hey Johnny, are you going to come over and have a look at what's on offer today?"

"Sorry Cody, we're in a bit of a hurry at the moment mate, maybe on the way back."

"Okay Johnny, see you soon," says Cody shrugging his shoulders.

As they cross in front of Second Avenue, by Doug's Fish and Chip Shop, they glance back and see that the bald man has come out of the church and is following them on foot, he is quite prominent in his black suit and sunglasses. They walk on at an even brisker pace than before. Resembling a couple of Olympic race walkers vying for the lead in a race, they are getting some strange looks from patrons of Doug's establishment as they pass by. Their buttocks are moving from side to side in unison as they pump their arms, which does look very comical. A young woman shouts out, "Bit cheeky" to Johnny and an old, bearded man says, "Nice arse" to Cherie.

They are getting more comments as they race walk past the Sandgate Fishmongers, receiving more giggles and banter from the patrons seated outside. As they approach 'Cremorne' there's a half a dozen kiteboarders skimming across the water on their boards opposite the house. The brightly coloured kites of green and gold, red and blue, black and orange, are zigzagging across the sky as the surfers do jumps and turns and other tricks on the water's surface, which is only about a metre deep at the present time. But this is not the time to be admiring their skills.

Cremorne was built in the early 20th century as a private residence for John McCallum a well-known film producer and actor. The house is now split into units and badly in need of some tender loving care, the tin roof is now very rusted, and the paintwork is flaking on the window frames. The Smith sisters live in the South Wing, as they call it, which has an unusual bay window. Cherie and Johnny have walked at a fast pace along Flinders Parade and are entering through the original brick archway with 'Cremorne' proudly displayed above it. They quickly go up the path to the left of the house then up some wooden steps that do not look too safe and knock on the door to the right of the bay window and as they wait for the door to open, their pursuer is getting ever closer. A flurry of activity can be heard inside the unit and just as the bald man reaches the 'Cremorne' entrance, the door to the unit opens and Millie and Tillie are standing there in their Sunday best with the happiest expression on their faces. Johnny and Cherie surprise the ladies by pushing past them to go inside the unit and slam the door shut behind them each with forced cheesy grins on their faces. The sisters are dressed almost identically in full-length lacy dresses with long sleeves and high collars, the only difference being that Millie's is Purple and Tillie's is Beige. They both give Johnny a big hug.

The Smith sisters have always been very fond of Johnny, their real names are Millicent and Matilda. Millicent taught Johnny Social Studies when he attended Shorncliffe Primary School. The sisters were also very good friends with his mother, as she had been a member of the school's P and C Committee and was a relief teacher there.

"You're a bit earlier than we had expected," says Tillie.

"Oh yes," says Johnny, "The service at the Baptist Church wasn't as long as we thought it was going to be." He grimaces and glances at Cherie, "Was it dear?" He can't believe that he said dear.

Cherie is trying to look out of the window and sees that their adversary is out of breath and leaning on the wall outside the property. "What... er... no, no... er... it was very short wasn't it darling," she says flummoxed and can't believe she said darling and rolls her eyes.

"Oh well, never mind," says Millie smiling, "We will have morning tea ready in no time, won't we Matilda?"

Matilda nods and the sisters are about to go into the back room to get things ready, when they both stop and give Johnny the kind of look his mother used to give him and they say in unison, "You seem to have forgotten your manners, Johnny?"

"Manners?" says Johnny confused. Cherie smiles and nudges him with her elbow and then points her finger towards the sisters and then back to herself. "Oh yes," he says, it's like his own mother is scolding him. "Sorry… this is my friend Cherie, Cherie this is Millie and Tillie, or to be correct Millicent and Matilda, the Smith sisters I told you about yesterday."

"I am very pleased to meet you both," says Cherie holding out her hand, but they ignore her hand, and both come rushing over and each give her the biggest hug.

"And we are pleased to meet you too my dear," they say as one.

"Now my dears," says Millie "Just make yourself comfortable in the back room."

"And we will go into the kitchen and get everything ready," pipes in Tillie.

"Hope you've both got a good appetite," says Millie.

"Yes, we've been baking all morning," adds Tillie.

Johnny and Cherie look at each other and nod to them enthusiastically, "Yes we're famished," they say in unison as if mimicking the sister's habit of speaking at the same time. They are certainly ready for a big feed, as they didn't get the opportunity to have that full Aussie breakfast at Cherie's place.

The sisters hurry into the kitchen and Johnny and Cherie both flop down wearily into a comfy-looking sofa in the living room, they hear a TV in the next room which is tuned in to a twenty-four-hour news channel.

"If he was a proper cop, he would have been knocking on the door by now," whispers Johnny.

"We could ring the police now on the old ladies' phone, because this is starting to become a little scary," adds Cherie looking very worried.

Just then, they both stand as they hear a news flash on the television in the other room:

"A man's body has been washed ashore on Amity beach on the northern part of Stradbroke Island. Local police are investigating the matter. The man is believed to be in his fifties, his body was discovered at about 6am this morning by some tourists visiting the area. The body has not been identified, but police say he was wearing a Bayern Munich Football Club jersey. First indications are that he may have fallen off a passing Tanker or Cargo ship and investigations are continuing with the crews of ships currently berthed at the Port of Brisban…"

"Oh my god," says Cherie, putting her hand to her mouth, "That sounds like Manfred… Manfred Muller, he sometimes helps Tony Pesaro on his trawler, he is German, only speaks a little English and he's a very proud Bayern Munich supporter and he often wears one of their soccer supporter tee shirts."

They are standing by the door to the room with the television and can see pictures of a covered-up body lying on Amity beach. "German?" says Johnny wondering and casts his mind back to the man in the grey hoodie that bashed Phillip, who told him that he had a foreign accent and was bitten by his greyhound, Kristal. The man had said "swine, hound" but it is more probable that he said "schweinehund" which means pig dog a vile insult in Germany. Johnny knew this, because he had done some German language in high school. "He must have been the guy that bashed Phil, he's probably been killed because he's stuffed up, he couldn't find the USB and now the contraband has gone missing, and he's become the fall guy. He hasn't drowned by falling off a ship about to enter the Port of Brisbane, he's been murdered, I'll bet he was probably thrown overboard from that trawler belonging to Tony Pesaro, and this guy outside must have ordered him to do it."

Just then the two sisters return, "Oh sorry we should have turned the television off when you arrived, nothing worth watching anyway," says Millie who puts down a tray holding a large tea pot, four bone-china teacups, saucers, side plates, milk and sugar onto a coffee table and goes and turns off the television. Tillie is holding a three-tiered cake stand which contains a most stupendous selection of lamingtons, cupcakes, Danish pastries, fruit scones, apple strudel, Vanilla slices and on the top tier a Pavlova, which she also places on the coffee table.

"I hope you are both hungry," enquires Millie.

"Oh yes," says Cherie, "You bet" confirms Johnny. After the overnight escapade and their recent race walk down Flinders Parade, they are both ravenous and begin to look quite comical as they proceed to devour almost every cake on the stand and they both wash it all down by drinking two cups of tea that the large teapot has provided. They look quite a sight with cream and jam on their faces and the sisters look at each other in amazement. They have never witnessed anything quite like it before from previous guests, but they are pleased that their efforts have been appreciated.

"Yes, we knew Johnny's mother," says Millie whilst the cakes are being devoured, "Such a lovely woman" adds Tillie. "She used to come round here quite often with Johnny on Sundays for tea and cakes, when he was a boy," Millie continues, "But that was when we occupied the whole house," "It was left to us by a relative," adds Tillie again. Johnny and Cherie just nod at them as they are munching cakes nonstop and drinking tea during this conversation. "Yes," Millie adds, "We have had to rent out the other rooms in the house, so we can make ends meet, it has been hard for us both at times."

"So how long have you two been together?" the sisters ask together.

"Err… about two days I suppose" answers Johnny, not knowing quite what to say and he embarrassingly looks to Cherie to back him up with his mouth half full.

"Two days!" exclaim the sisters again speaking at the same time, "Is that all."

"Yes, but it seems much longer doesn't it Johnny?" says Cherie, smiling to herself as she mops the cream and jam from her mouth with a hand-made napkin.

"Oh yes, definitely," says Johnny "It's been quite an adventure for us both so far, hasn't it dear?"

Cherie stares at Johnny, then stands and changes the subject. "Ladies, do you mind if I use your phone?"

"Phone?" says Millie. "Oh, sorry Cherie, it's out of order, I'm sorry to say," adds Tillie.

Cherie and Johnny look at each other, they are crest fallen.

"But don't worry, you can use our neighbour's phone if it is an urgent matter," says Tillie, "Just knock on his door, it's the apartment at the back, it's number 2." Cherie is shown a door at the back of the flat. "Just tell the young man who lives there that we sent you round, he won't mind at all."

Cherie gives Johnny a pointed look and goes out into the small back garden, he knows that she is going to call the police now and he can't argue with that as it is probably the best thing to do in the circumstances. There's a man outside the front of the house with a gun and Johnny doesn't want the Smith sisters to be endangered by all this business, especially after hearing about the German man's death.

"She's lovely," says Millie after Cherie had gone.

"Yes, I like to see a girl with a healthy appetite," adds Tillie with glee.

"Oh, I must apologize for our manners ladies," says Johnny, "We had quite a torrid time last night and haven't been able to have any breakfast yet."

"Torrid!" the sisters say at the same time, looking very shocked.

He realises what they must be thinking, "Oh no, no, not that... err... bad choice of words... we just had a really physical night that's all."

"Physical!" they say in unison, looking even more horrified now.

"No, no ladies, you misunderstand, we've just been paddling... yes... paddling, right, in a kayak... very strenuous," says Johnny desperately making a paddling motion.

"Ohhh," say the sisters together, looking at each other in relief, "Well no wonder you were hungry," adds Millie and they both smile at Johnny.

Chapter 18

CHERIE IS GONE

After a few minutes, Johnny wonders what is taking Cherie so long, he goes to the bay window and checks the front of the house but can't see the bald man outside anymore, he comes back into the living room thinking that Cherie should have returned by now. He excuses himself again and goes out the back door into the garden and walks up to the rear apartment. He knocks on No. 2's door and it is opened by a long-haired, unshaven young man who seems annoyed saying, "Who is it this time?" Johnny looks surprised and asks him if Cherie has finished making her phone call yet. The young man looks confused and says, "Phone call, what phone call… are you having me on mate?"

"The Smith sisters just sent her round," says Johnny perplexed, "Said you would let her use the phone."

He shrugs his shoulders and says, "The sisters?" looks up at the back door of their house and continues, "Oh yeah… them, no mate, nobody's been round here, but somebody did knock on the door a few minutes ago, but when I opened it, there was nobody there."

Johnny goes cold, he doesn't say anything further but runs around the side of the building and through the 'Cremorne' entrance, looks up and down Flinders Parade, but can't see any sign of Cherie or for that matter the bald man in the black suit who was standing outside Cremorne before. All he notices is a boy pedalling towards him on a BMX bike. The sisters have now come out of their front door and have joined Johnny on the footpath.

"What's the matter Johnny?" says Millie concerned.

"Where's Cherie gone?" asks Tillie, putting her hand on Johnny's arm.

"They've got her!" Johnny cries out frantically "Cherie's been taken!"

Chapter 19

A HOSTAGE IS TAKEN

Cherie walks up to Unit No.2 and knocks on the door when a large hairy tanned hand suddenly covers her mouth tightly and before she realises what is happening, she is being picked up and carried out through a side entrance of the property and out onto the footpath in Seventh Avenue where a cream coloured van is parked with its back door open. Although she cannot see his face, she knows it's Tony Pesaro who is carrying her, as he has a fishy smell coming from him. She tries to shout out to Johnny, but Tony's hand is so tight around her mouth she is having trouble even breathing. After Tony bundles her into the back of the van, the bald man who is waiting on the footpath gets into the back and sits on top of her pushing a beretta pistol into her ribs warning her not to move or cry out.

"I came as quick as I could boss," says Tony as he gets into the driver's seat and drives off travelling south along Flinders Parade.

"Well, you are not out of trouble yet Tony," his boss replies and then after only travelling a short distance he says, "Pull over here." They are opposite the Sandgate Fishmongers near the swimming pool.

"Probably not a good time to eat boss?" says Tony.

"Fool!" he replies and takes out a notebook, scribbles a message onto a page, rips it out folds it in half and gives it to Tony with a ten dollar note saying, "See that kid on the BMX bike outside the fish and chip shop?" Tony nods. "Give him ten bucks and tell him to deliver this note to Mr. Blakemore at Unit No.1 at the 'Cremorne' building." While Tony is doing as he is instructed, Cherie cries out pathetically, because the weight of the man on her body is really beginning to cause her pain. The bald man raises the beretta threatening to hit her, thinks better of it and instead slaps her on the side of her head violently with his open hand stunning her into silence and he says, "Keep quiet and stay still." While she is groaning in semi-consciousness, he grabs some black masking tape that is lying in the back of the van, tears off two strips and covers her mouth and eyes. Tony gets back into the van saying, "I did what you told me Boss." He's still sitting on Cherie and asks Tony if he has anything to tie her up with, so Tony grabs some cable ties from inside his glove box. The bald man then orders Tony to drive back to the church and using the cable ties he secures Cherie's hands behind her and binds her ankles together as well.

When they get to Cliff Street by the Baptist Church, the boss gets out of the back of the van, slams the door shut, goes to the drivers' side window and gives Tony some instructions. All Cherie can catch from this conversation is, "Don't stuff it up!" The boss then collects his car and drives off. Tony drives down Cliff Street and Cherie begins to roll around aggressively in the back of the van trying to get free. The cable ties are cutting into her wrists and ankles, causing her even more pain. Tony shouts over his shoulder "Quedate quieto!"

After driving for only a few minutes, Tony stops the van, but the motor is still running. Cherie can hear him pulling up a roller door, then he gets back into the van and drives a few metres forward and then she hears him pulling the roller doors back down again. The rear door of the van opens, and she is dragged out onto a concrete floor by Tony and Ronny who must have been waiting for them to arrive. Cherie suffers grazes to her knees as they drag her along. Then Ronny closes the roller doors and Tony pulls Cherie onto her feet, manhandles her into a room and because she is tied up by the wrists and ankles she drops helplessly to the floor and then manages to move herself into a sitting down position. Tony notices a large bruise is starting to become visible on the right side of her jaw, and he surmises that the boss must have struck her whilst he was giving the boy on the BMX the message for Johnny Blakemore.

Tony crouches by Cherie's side and puts his hand on the side of her face inspecting her injury saying, "El Bruto," but she moves her head away violently and mumbles something that he can't understand. He pulls the masking tape from her mouth, which causes her to shriek with pain and she says, "I know it's you Tony, I can smell the fish on you, you'll never get away with this you know."

Tony says, "You've made a big mistake Cherie, if we don't get that stuff back, this man will kill both of us and your boyfriend as well, so for all our sakes you had better tell us where it is."

"If you kill me, you won't get any of it back will you and I'm not going to tell you where it is unless you let me go. We've hidden it in a place where you'll never find it."

"Oh yes we will," says Tony. "Because your boyfriend won't want anything to happen to you, he'll tell us where it is alright."

"Not if you harm me, he won't," says Cherie defiantly, "And another thing, I know you killed Manfred, how could you do that, he was your friend?"

Tony closes his eyes, and he thinks for a moment then says softly, "I didn't kill him Cherie, I've never killed anyone in my life, please believe me when I say that" and he replaces the masking tape back onto her mouth. Cherie slumps forward, she is fatigued and wants to close her eyes and have some rest after all the trauma of being manhandled, smacked on the jaw and held hostage. She still hasn't managed to get any sleep after the night before. Tony looks down at her, he feels guilty, he never wanted this to happen. He then takes out his mobile phone, dials a number, closes the door to the room and goes back to where his van is parked. He says into his phone, "Boss, you shouldn't have hit her, you could have caused her permanent damage."

"Damage? Tony we are all going to be damaged if we don't get the stuff back, it's your job now to just keep trying to find out what she knows."

"Oh, she knows where it is for sure boss, but she won't tell me anything except that they've hidden it somewhere. But he'll tell us where it is, won't he? If he wants to get his girlfriend back in one piece."

"Keep working on her," he replies sternly, "Let me worry about the boyfriend, you keep working on her. Break her arm if you must, but we have to find the stuff. We have to get it back, because if we don't, as I said before, both of us will be more than damaged."

"Okay boss, I'll do my best," says Tony.

"No, Tony, do your worst!" He hangs up.

Tony looks at his mobile phone for a few seconds and says under his breath, "Hijo de puta."

Chapter 20

JOHNNY IN A HURRY

The boy on the BMX bike brakes hard as he reaches Johnny and the sisters, holding out the note given to him by Tony Pesaro and says, "Are you Mr. Blakemore?" Johnny nods, "A man asked me to give this to you."

Johnny takes the note and reads it out to himself:

DO NOT GO TO THE POLICE
GO STRAIGHT HOME
YOU WILL BE CONTACTED ON YOUR LANDLINE

He thinks for a few seconds and then grabs the handlebars of the boy's bike saying, "Can I borrow your bike?" The boy is shocked, he plants his feet firmly on the ground, holds on to his bike tightly and refuses to get off or let go.

"Johnny!" say the sisters in unison scolding him.

"Oh, sorry son," says Johnny regretting his actions. He turns to the sisters saying, "Sorry ladies' emergency, need to get home quickly." He starts running south along Flinders Parade towards the Baptist church. He crosses Third Avenue at full pace, luckily no cars are there, a little further along as he runs past Doug's establishment, he nearly collides with a patron carrying a par-cel of fish and chips, who angrily shouts at him, "Hey you bugger!" Johnny looks back at him and doesn't notice a car turning from Flinders Parade into Second Avenue at the roundabout. He almost gets run over as the car comes to a sudden halt with the driver sounding the horn loudly.

As he runs past First Avenue, opposite the Pop-Up Artists once again, he is again spotted by Cody Black who calls out, "Hey, not coming over today then?" Johnny is too focused on running as fast as he can and doesn't reply, and a frustrated Cody throws his arms up into the air in amazement.

When Johnny rounds the corner into Cliff Street, Cherie's yellow Suzuki is still parked there, but the green Mini Cooper is not in sight. He pulls her driver's door open, but he remembers that Cherie still has her spare car key. He slams the door shut and runs up the steep path that leads to the Full Moon Hotel on Eagle Terrace. When he arrives at the top of the hill, he is breathless, stops and drops down onto his haunches with his hands on his knees and says, "I'm getting too old for this type of caper." He thinks for a few seconds and takes in the scene in front of him. There are a group of cyclists sitting outside the hotel having a drink and their bikes are leaning against the pub wall. He moves across the street at speed and grabs one of the bicycles, hopping astride it and shouts to them, "Sorry guys, emergency, just borrowing it for a short while, I will bring it back later." He begins freewheeling down Curlew Street, which is a very steep hill. The cyclist whose bike has been stolen shouts angrily, "Come back you bastard!" Some of the other cyclists decide to chase after him in pursuit, which is a bit tricky as they are all wearing those clunky road shoes that cyclists wear to fit into their pedals. They look like a group of clog dancers as they comically bump into each other attempting to mount their bikes. This gives Johnny a good head start, but he hasn't figured out how to put his own feet into the bike's pedals yet, and he is quickly picking up speed as he rattles down the hill and straight across Rainbow Street, causing a couple of vehicles travelling in opposite directions to brake hard to avoid him. "Idiot!" shouts one of the drivers, "Moron" chimes in the other, both giving him a two-finger salute out of their open windows. The other cyclists are now in hot pursuit of the bike thief but come to an abrupt halt as the two cars that narrowly missed Johnny are blocking their direct route across Rainbow Street. Johnny hasn't figured out how the brakes work on the bike yet, but he has managed to get his toes into the pedals enabling him to pedal furiously to escape his pursuers. As he continues towards Curlew Park, he approaches a railway crossing which has its lights flashing, warning of an approaching train and the barriers are already down. Johnny doesn't slow down but traverses the railway crossing by swerving around the barrier and closes his eyes as he hears the frantic tooting sounds of the train's horn. He can feel the bicycle's wheels bumping along the rails and senses the closeness of the train as it flashes past him. The wind draught from the train has almost caused Johnny to be swept off the bike. He opens his eyes whilst still pedalling and knows he has had a miraculous escape by making it across the train track unscathed. His adrenalin is high, and he shouts out joyously, "Thank you Queensland Rail!" The cyclists who were in hot pursuit are arriving at the railway crossing but are unable to carry on their chase for the time being, due to the railway crossing gate barring their way. They angrily shout more obscenities from the other side of the tracks and violently shake their fists and make crude gestures at him.

Johnny continues pedalling as fast as he can and when he gets to the other side of Curlew Park, he continues along the concrete path that runs between the Dog Park and the Footy fields. A football appears out of the sky and bounces just in front of him, it has been kicked by a youth competing in a game of junior rugby league currently in progress. When he gets to Ashford Street, he alights the bicycle and leaves it lying at the edge of the park, thinking that the cyclists may not pursue him any further once the bike is back with its owner. A crackle of cockatoos is now swirling around the park, giving out their loud raucous calls, which seems to fit in with the situation Johnny has found himself in. He starts running down Wharf Street past a historic home which the locals have nicknamed the Wedding Cake House and turns the corner into Palm Avenue where his car is parked outside Cherie's house. He goes round to her back door, which is not locked and retrieves his bunch of keys and his mobile that was left on her kitchen table the night before. He looks out of the front window and can see that a group of cyclists are milling around at the bottom of Palm Avenue, obviously searching for him. He waits for them to ride off up Palm Avenue and out of sight, before picking up Cherie's bunch of keys and her mobile. After making sure all her doors are locked, he leaves her home and gets into his own car. He drives along Sinbad Street and slows down slightly as he passes the Santa Maria trawler. He notices that the white van is no longer parked there, but Ronny is there busying himself on the trawler. He speeds up as he passes the disused co-op buildings as he knows he must get home quickly, before the expected phone call on his landline.

On arrival at Jetty Street, Johnny goes inside, lets Misty in from the back, puts the two sets of keys and Cherie's mobile on the coffee table, plugs his own mobile into a charger and then is horrified as he notices he has a message on his landline. His heart sinks, as he assumes he hasn't made it home in time to pick up the receiver for the promised phone call and tentatively pushes the message button and listens. "Hi Johnny, Mike Murphy here mate, look I don't know if you heard, but a man has drowned on Stradbroke Island and his description fits the one that you and Mr. Phillips gave us on Friday, could you please come down to the station at nine o'clock tomorrow morning, just need you to make a formal statement about what you saw, thanks mate."

After ringing Sergeant Murphy on his mobile, Johnny agrees to be at the Police Station at 9am Monday morning to make a formal statement, but he doubts he will be keeping this appointment. While waiting for the expected phone call from Cherie's kidnappers, Johnny makes himself a large mug of coffee as he is so tired, but desperate to stay awake. He slumps down into an armchair next to his landline and is beginning to nod off when he is startled by the phone ringing, and seeing it's an unlisted number, he answers immediately. "So, you made it back?" says a man in a deep educated voice.

"Where's Cherie, you bastard! You had better not have hurt her."

"That depends on you Johnny, doesn't it? Just tell me where the stuff is, and she won't be harmed."

"Really, we know you had that German guy killed, so what's to stop you killing Cherie after I tell you where it is?"

The man thinks for a moment and says in a quiet but deliberate voice, "You'll just have to trust me, won't you Johnny?"

"Trust you! You bastard, you've got to be kidding me, I'm only going to tell you where the stuff is, after I am certain that Cherie is safe."

"I hope the stuff is safe too Johnny, for both your sakes."

"Well then, you'll just have to trust me, won't you?" replies Johnny triumphantly, "Set Cherie free and I'll tell you where I hid the stuff."

There is a long pause, Johnny can hear breathing on the other end of the phone, and then the man says, "I'll call you again, you just think about things Johnny, stay in your house and don't be stupid, because if you call the police, I'll find out that you did and then who knows what might happen to your precious girlfriend."

The man hangs up, "Hello, Hello," Johnny slams down his phone. He is wide awake now, but he is very distraught, he doesn't know what to do for the best, he wants to go out and look for Cherie but is worried that if they find out he's left the house and doesn't answer the landline when it rings, there may be consequences for Cherie. He is still loath to get the police involved at this stage as the bald man in the black suit may be a bent cop or has some other cops in his pay, and because he did say he will find out about it if Johnny should call the police.

Johnny spends the afternoon just sitting in his armchair wondering what he should do next as he waits for another phone call. His dog Misty senses that something is wrong and places her head on his lap and he is patting her, which gives him a little comfort. The time is now 5pm and he has just about made up his mind about what to do when his mobile rings, the screen shows that it's Danny, he lets it ring a few times not wanting to answer, in case the mysterious man might ring him simultaneously on his landline. Eventually he picks up the call, "Hello Danny."

"Johnny? Hi mate, hey I guess you are getting on alright with Cherie heh?" Johnny doesn't answer. "Well, she didn't come to rehearsals this afternoon at the theatre, and she isn't answering her phone and that's most unlike her. Mandy and I thought that she was probably with you having a good time, you crafty bugger."

Johnny looks at Cherie's mobile phone on the coffee table which probably needs to be re-charged. "Cherie? Oh no, no idea mate," he says lying, "I did see her on Saturday morning, we went to the Town Hall Café for tea and scones, but she had to go to work, and I haven't seen or spoken to her since mate."

"But you did hit it off okay didn't you because Jack saw her car outside your house on Saturday night, the yellow Suzuki right and I bumped into Cody Black from SasArt earlier, who said he saw you when he was working at the Pop-Up Artists this morning, and he thought you were both acting very strange. He said you were walking very fast after you both left the Baptist church and later you ran past him going the opposite way."

"Oh, the spies are out, are they?" replies Johnny sharply, wanting Daniel to stop asking him questions, "Look I've got to go now Danny, okay?"

"Oh, okay then mate… sorry… look, are you okay Johnny, you don't sound your usual chirpy self."

"I'm fine!" he replies sharply. Then much softer, "Danny I'm fine, look I'm sorry to be so short with you, but I'm expecting an important phone call, I'll have to finish our conversation now, okay?"

"Oh, alright Johnny, another film offer I suppose?"

"Yeah Danny, something like that," and Johnny hangs up.

A few minutes later, his mobile rings again, it's a Queensland landline phone number that he doesn't recognise, so not sure who it might be he answers, "Yes?"

"Oh Johnny, thank heavens you are alright, we're using our neighbour's phone, very good of him," it's Millie Smith. "We've been so worried about you and Cherie," adds Tillie. "You said

Cherie was taken," it's Millie again. "What did you mean by taken, Johnny?" says Tillie finishing her sentence again.

"Taken?" answers Johnny, "Err... taken ill, she was taken ill, yes that's it."

"Oh," says Millie, "But you also said she's gone, Johnny." Tillie finishes the sentence again, "What did you mean by gone?"

"Erm... says Johnny, "Well she was taken ill and so she's gone to see the doctor, yes that's it, gone to see the doctor, he gave her some tablets, she had a terrible migraine you know, but she's alright now, gone to bed early, ha, ha, ha, she'll be fine in the morning, okay?"

"Yes, well okay," says Millie, "Hope she's well soon," adds Tillie. "Give her our love," they say together.

Johnny says, "Bye" and hangs up, before they can ask him any more questions.

At the other end of the phone, after Johnny has hung up, Millie says to Tillie, "But doctors don't open on a Sunday, do they?"

Johnny's mobile phone starts ringing again and this time he does recognise the caller.

Chapter 21

CHERIE TAKES IT ON THE CHIN

Cherie had fallen asleep due to her exhaustive state and is now starting to wake up. She is lying on a cold concrete floor, every muscle in her body aches and has no idea where she is or how long she might have been lying there. Her jaw is throbbing intensely from the blow that the boss inflicted on her and she has a blinding headache, well it would be blinding if she could see anything, her eyes are still covered with the masking tape. Cherie wants to put her hand to her cheek but can't because her hands are tied behind her back. She is still only wearing the capri slacks and AC/DC T-shirt, belonging to Sophie that Johnny loaned her earlier and she is still wearing her own boat shoes. Cherie is shivering because of being cold and works out that the sun must be going down or already has. The cable ties have cut into her wrists and ankles. She can't see anything, because of the masking tape over her eyes, but because Tony didn't re-apply the masking tape to her mouth properly, she can breathe more easily via her mouth as well as her nose, giving her a little relief. Although she is probably able to, she decides not to cry out for help, not yet anyway, as Tony will figure out the masking tape needs replacing. No, much better to wait for the right opportunity before she brings her plight to anyone's attention. Moving a few inches at a time, using a lot of her strength, Cherie manages to shuffle her way across the concrete floor until she reaches a wall on the other side of the room. She manages to get herself into a sitting position with her back against the wall.

Where am I? she thinks, "Where's Johnny?" she says quietly, and thinking again, why doesn't he call the police? But he doesn't know where I am, does he? So many questions. She is also wondering what is going to happen to her, thinking of the worst possible scenario, will they really kill me? Is the black plastic package they located near Mud Island really that valuable, is it so important that they are prepared to kill her for it? But they killed Manfred, didn't they? So, the answer is yes. Cherie is trying to think logically now and work out where she might be located. Even though it is very quiet, there is the occasional sound of a car passing by, so she must be near a road with traffic. Her spirits are raised when she hears a familiar sound. It is a toot of a horn, and then after another 30 seconds she hears another toot, not a car horn but the toot that a train horn makes. She knows that familiar sound, it's the sound that the Shorncliffe train makes as it approaches each of the railway crossings at Curlew Park and Palm Avenue during the train's journey between Sandgate and Shorncliffe. Cherie now knows she is close to home; she is still in Shorncliffe or Sandgate and manages to relax a little raising a slight smile underneath the masking tape covering her mouth.

Chapter 22

THE LINKS LEAD TO
A DISCOVERY

The time is now 6:30pm on Sunday evening and it's starting to get dark outside, Misty hasn't had a walk all day and she's getting restless. Johnny hasn't received another call from the boss, so he decides to bite the bullet and take Misty for a stroll and see if he can find out anything at the trawler site in Sinbad Street. He intends to confront Tony, if he can find him and locate where they might be holding Cherie. He also wants to find out if Tony has taken the Santa Maria out prawn trawling that evening, as it's possible Cherie might be on board. Oh my god, he thinks, they wouldn't do to her what they did to the German guy would they?

Johnny now has Misty on her leash, and he is walking down Allpass Parade underneath the huge fig trees to avoid being seen by any passing cars. He decides to enter the Golf Club grounds via the car park and walk past the clubhouse of this century old golf course that was built on a salt pan and marshy ground. The golf course is only nine holes due to the unavailability of land in this area. They walk down the middle of the ninth fairway towards the ninth tee. The course is closed now, so no need to worry about stray golf balls. As they approach the green of the eighth fairway, Johnny sees a light shining through a window in the old Sandgate

Fisherman's Co-Operative Society building. Wondering who could be in there on a Sunday night, he and Misty go through a gap in the wire fence that circumnavigates the golf course. They are now on a large piece of vacant land between Sinbad Street and the edge of the golf course. Johnny is hidden well enough from view because there is no lighting away from the road or on the golf course. They slowly edge their way through some long grass, arriving at some trees closer to the road, giving them some cover and a better chance of not being spotted by passing traffic. The Santa Maria is still moored at the dock, but there is no sign of any activity on the boat now. Johnny wonders why there is a light on in the Fisherman's Co-op building, who could be in there? He cannot see Tony's Van parked there, but if it's parked inside the building, maybe he will be able to confront him and find out where they are holding Cherie.

Johnny ties Misty's leash to the tree giving them cover, making sure no cars are approaching from either direction, and he quickly crosses Sinbad Street to the co-op and stops when he gets to the wire fence surrounding the building. He finds it a hard struggle but manages to climb over the wire fence. Out of breath, he drops to the ground on the other side and moves quickly to a roller door at the front of the building, which is locked. There is a window about two and a half metres off the ground, so too high for Johnny to be able to look inside. He searches around and finds an old crate nearby and turns it on its side which enables him to stand upon it to gain some extra height. He looks in the window and Tony's Van is parked inside. Tony is pacing up and down holding his mobile phone, but there is no sign of Cherie.

Johnny hops down off the crate, thinks for a minute, picks up the crate and goes to the rear side of the building where there is another window also about two and a half metres above the ground. He places the crate in the same position as before, climbs onto it and is overjoyed, but also shocked as he can see Cherie sitting on the floor with her back to the opposite wall. Her hands and feet appear to be shackled in some sort of way and her head is tilted sideways between her knees, clearly showing that her eyes and mouth have tape across them.

He wants to cry out to her but sensibly thinks better of it. The bastards, he thinks, they've hurt her, they are not going to get away with this. He reluctantly leaves, making his way back over the wire fence surrounding the co-op building, crossing Sinbad Street. Misty is patiently lying on the ground next to the tree waiting for him. Johnny dials a number on his mobile phone, Danny answers and Johnny says, "Right mate, what we talked about earlier, did you manage to get everyone up to speed… good, I've got to get back home as quick as I can, but I'll ring you very shortly with a plan."

Chapter 23

A CUNNING PLAN

After jogging back to his place in Jetty Street, it is 8pm and as Johnny enters his front door, his landline is ringing. He rushes to his phone and sees the caller is an unlisted number, he snatches up the receiver hoping that no one has rung whilst he is away from his home, "Yes," he says breathing hard.

"Oh, good boy Johnny," answers the boss, "You are still there, but you sound a little upset, I hope you've had some time to reflect on all this and you have decided to cooperate with us?"

"Yes," replies Johnny, "As long as you don't harm Cherie, I will tell you how you can get your stuff back."

"No, Johnny, of course we haven't harmed her, now where is the stuff!"

You are a liar thinks Johnny, finding it hard to control his emotions, but he manages to keep calm by saying "Okay, meet me at Baxter's Jetty, but come in your trawler. Yes, I know about the trawler, no cars, I want to make sure that you are all in the trawler, okay, so there's no funny business. That's you, Tony Pesaro and the other guy. We will all go and get the stuff together, but we will need a trawler to do it, let's say 9:30pm okay?"

"Very good, Johnny, you are learning fast, but don't tell any-one else about this, especially the police, or I will find out, you know that I will, don't you? And then it will be curtains for you and your girlfriend. So don't even think about trying any funny business. Do you understand me?"

"Yes, I understand perfectly," says Johnny with a smirk on his face, "See you at 9:30pm then?"

"Looking forward to it Johnny," replies the boss smugly and hangs up.

Johnny picks up his mobile phone and rings Danny and when he answers he begins by saying, "Okay mate it's on, this is what I want you all to do."

Chapter 24

A CLEVER DIVERSION

It is now 9pm on Sunday night and Johnny has returned to the co-op building on foot, but without Misty this time. He decided to leave his car at Jetty Street, his reasoning being that if it was spotted it might alert someone to the fact that he had left his house giving away where he was. He is standing under the same tree that he tied Misty to earlier, but this time he is carrying a small step ladder. There is some activity on the Santa Maria next to the co-op, Tony Pesaro has started the trawler's engine, and Ronny is on board also, but he can't see anyone else. There should be three of them as agreed, he wonders if the mystery bald man is trying to trick him. There is nothing Johnny can do about it now except to advise Danny. He makes a quick phone call warning him to be on the lookout for a bald man who drives a green Mini Cooper. Johnny waits until the Santa Maria is underway and is moving past the marina towards the channel; he then swiftly crosses the road and throws the step ladder over the wire fence which he struggles to climb over again. This time he lands on the other side of the fence awkwardly, slightly injuring his ankle and falling to the ground in some pain. Nevertheless, he picks himself up, grabs the ladder, and hobbles to the window at the side of the building. He places the step ladder under the window and when he climbs up, he can see that Cherie is still slumped in a sitting position with her back against the opposite wall. So, he takes a torch out of his jacket and uses it to break the glass in the window, calling out "Cherie!"

Cherie has been sleeping but wakes on hearing Johnny's voice. She attempts to sit up and calls out as best she can, "Oh Johnny, thank god you're here." However, she cannot be understood clearly due to the masking tape still covering her mouth.

The step ladder has given Johnny a much higher position next to the window than he had standing on a crate. He manages to get his body through the small window but receives lacerations to his hands from the broken glass in the process. This makes it difficult for Johnny to hang onto the window ledge on the inside of the building and he falls clumsily on his back onto the concrete floor below knocking the wind out of himself momentarily. "Oh shit!" he gasps.

"Are you alright Johnny," pleads Cherie meekly, not knowing what is happening. "Be careful Tony is in the next room."

"No, he's not," says Johnny as he breathlessly crawls alongside Cherie. He gently touches the side of her head and kisses her tenderly on her forehead. "Tony thinks he's meeting me at Baxter's Jetty at this very moment."

Using a Stanley knife he has taken from his pocket; Johnny cuts the cable ties that are securing Cherie's wrists and ankles and gently removes the masking tape from her mouth and eyes trying not to cause her any pain. She has trouble adjusting to the fluorescent light at first, but after focusing and making out Johnny's face she says, "What took you so long?" Then they both close their eyes and gently kiss, their lips hardly touching. "Mmm, maybe I should get taken hostage more often," she whispers jokingly.

Johnny's eyes suddenly open, "Come on, we haven't much time, we have to get out of here before they come back."

"Where the hell are we anyway?" asks Cherie looking around.

"Didn't you know? This is the old Fisherman's Co-Op Building; I had no idea it was still being used."

"Of course," nods Cherie, "I knew I wasn't far from my home, because I could hear the toots of the trains, but I didn't think that I was merely a couple of hundred metres away."

"Yeah, good old Queensland rail eh, they've helped us a couple of times today," says Johnny thinking about his previous two escapes via the railway crossings from the bald man in his mini and the group of angry cyclists.

They both manage to struggle to their feet; Johnny is limping slightly from his injured ankle and Cherie doesn't feel much better as she has a cramp in both her legs from being tied up and sitting on a concrete floor for practically half of the day.

"Don't you think we should call the police now Johnny?" Cherie implores him.

Johnny looks tenderly into her eyes and says softly "Now I know that you are safe, yes okay, I'll ring the police." He dials Mike Murphy's mobile number, but there is no reply, so he leaves a detailed message explaining everything that has happened and urges him to get some of his force down to the co-op building as quickly as possible and help them, as it's probably only a matter of time before they are discovered and who knows what might happen to them if they are. After the call, they wait confidently expecting that they will be rescued soon. At the other end of that phone call, Sergeant Murphy is sitting at his desk in a darkened office at the Sandgate Police Station looking very uncomfortable as his phone is ringing and seeing that the call is from Johnny Blakemore, he is not picking up.

Chapter 25

TRICKERY AT
BAXTER'S WHARF

It is now approaching 9:30 pm and the green Mini Cooper has been waiting for a few minutes in the car park next to Baxter's Jetty, the boss is sitting inside. The lights of the Santa Maria can now be seen coming up the channel as it passes the Volunteer Marine Rescue Dock on its way towards Baxter's Jetty. The area on the foreshore is deserted now, except for a figure holding a fishing rod standing on Baxter's Jetty. The fisherman is dangling his line in the water, it is high tide. The boss assumes this figure is Johnny and he's asked for the trawler because he intends to take them to where the large black package of drugs is located, but he is mistaken. It is not Johnny on Baxter's Jetty, it is Danny dressed in grey jogging pants, a checked flannelette shirt and wearing a black beanie. The two lifelong friends have hatched a plan between them to give Johnny enough time to rescue Cherie back at the co-op. After receiving Johnny's warning phone call that there are only two people on the trawler, not three as there should have been, Danny is alerted to a green mini in the car park. The boss gets out of his car and walks straight towards the angler, just as the Santa Maria is slowing next to Baxter's Jetty. Another figure appears from the rear of the toilet block adjacent to the car park, he is wearing a dark blue helmet, waving his arms and sprouting Shakespeare.

"To be or not to be, that is the question. Whether it is nobler in the mind to suffer the slings and arrows of outrageous fortune………" it's Shakespeare, well young Jack Hollis that is.

"Get out of here you bloody idiot!" The boss yells at Jack, while at the same time he is reaching inside his suit pocket, threatening to pull out his gun, "Or you'll be in big trouble."

Jack doesn't need a second invitation to leave, and he exclaims, "Exit stage right!" and sprints away up the hill and across Allpass Parade to where he left his electric scooter parked on the pavement. He jumps onto the E-scooter and takes off down Sunday Street and out of sight.

The boss grumbles as he watches him leave, "Fucking idiot!" and turns back towards the Jetty, but he can no longer see the person with the fishing rod. The distraction caused by Jack's theatrics has allowed Danny enough time to disappear. He is now clinging to a wooden pillar underneath the Jetty. Tony, who was also distracted by Jack, shouts over to the boss, "The prick who was fishing has pissed off!" and Ronny adds, "We've been tricked boss!"

The boss, who is now standing on the jetty, sees a fishing rod lying on the wooden deck, but he doesn't notice Danny who is desperately clinging on to one of the pillars immediately below him. The boss is fuming and shouts back to the trawler, "You should have kept an eye on him, anyway, I'm certain it wasn't Johnny Blakemore with the fishing rod. Something very strange is going on here, it must have been a trick to distract us. I don't like it, look I'm going back to the co-op, you two get back there with the trawler as quick as you can."

"Okay boss," replies Tony, but turning a Prawn Trawler around in this narrow channel will take some skill and a little time to achieve, but he doesn't divulge that to his boss.

The boss quickly returns to his car, muttering to himself and his phone rings, he recognises the caller. "Yes!" he says sternly putting the phone to his ear listening to what the caller has to say, "Oh really, how long ago was this… well, he is going to be very sorry that he crossed me, very sorry indeed, look all you need to do is keep out of it and don't do anything, okay." After hanging up, the boss gets into his car and pulls a silencer out of the glove box clicking it into place onto the barrel of the Beretta pistol that he had in his inside suit pocket. He starts his engine and the mini races out of the car park and down Allpass Parade heading towards the co-op.

Meanwhile back at Sandgate Police Station, Sergeant Mike Murphy is in his office looking remorseful as he stares at his mobile phone on his desk in front of him. He's listening to Johnny's message which begins, "Hey Spud, it's Blakey mate, need your help urgently…"

Chapter 26

DOWN IN THE BOONDALL WETLANDS

Johnny and Cherie are concerned that the police have not yet arrived to rescue them. They have tried to open the roller door at the front of the building, but it is firmly locked. Johnny's hands are bleeding and feeling painful due to him cutting them badly when getting through the broken window. They cannot escape the same way that Johnny entered, as the window is too high for them to reach from the inside of the building and there is nothing suitable to stand on. They know it will not be long before they are both discovered, and this is endorsed when Johnny's phone rings, it's a call from Danny who is still clinging to a jetty pillar. Danny lets Johnny know that the green mini is heading their way, and in return Johnny advises Danny that he has left a message with Sergeant Mike Murphy. After the phone call, Johnny and Cherie focus their attention on the rear door to the co-op building and are relieved when they manage to get it open. They go through the door which leads out onto a deck. However, the high wire fence that surrounds the co-op building extends all the way round to each end of the dock. They are contemplating how they might be able to climb over or around the wire fence, when they notice the headlights of the green Mini Cooper hurtling up the road towards them. The car skids to a sudden halt outside the front of the co-op building. There is nothing else for them to do but to make a leap of faith and jump into Cabbage Tree Creek. They need to swim across to the opposite side and try and make it to the Boondall Wetlands and hopefully safety, well for a while at least.

Meanwhile, Tony has used his maritime skills to turn the Santa Maria around in the channel and the trawler is heading back down Cabbage Tree Creek towards the co-op. The boss has his pistol in one hand as he pulls up the roller door of the co-op with his other, and straightaway sees that Cherie is no longer tied up on the floor. A window has been smashed and there's broken glass and blood stains on the ground. He now knows he has been tricked, there has been an intruder, and it was obviously Johnny. Seeing that the door to the dock is open and hearing noises coming from the deck area, the boss thinks, I've got them, they are trapped.

Johnny and Cherie hold hands and simultaneously jump into the cold water and start swimming across the creek, as the boss enters the dock area. On hearing the large splash, he runs out to the edge of the dock with his pistol in hand. Using the light coming from the doorway of the dock, he can easily make out two shapes swimming in the water towards the opposite side of the creek, he raises his pistol and fires one shot at them, but immediately after pulling the trigger it suddenly dawns on him that he needs them to be alive or he won't be able to find out where the contraband is. On hearing the dull gunshot Johnny feels the buzz of the bullet passing close to his ear, resembling an annoying insect. They both see the bullet impact on the water in front of them and duck down instinctively beneath the surface of the creek. They swim underwater for a few metres until their feet touch the muddy bank on the other side of the creek. Johnny holds onto Cherie's hand tightly to stop her from leaving the creek and indicates that it would be safer for them to make their way slowly along the riverbank with their heads just above the water. When they hear the chugging of the Santa Maria passing close by, they again duck down under the water's surface to ensure that they are not spotted. Tony and Ronny on board the trawler haven't noticed them in the water and Tony is only now being informed by the boss by phone about what has happened. After trudging along the muddy bank and resisting the urge to climb out of the creek, Johnny and Cherie continue wading along the creek shoreline. They reach the bird hide at the junction of Cabbage Tree and Nundah Creeks, where they know it will be easier for them to go ashore into the safety of the Boondall Wetlands Park opposite the public boat ramp. It is too dark for them to be seen where they are now, but what Johnny and Cherie can't understand is why they haven't heard any police sirens yet, it must be a good 20 to 30 minutes since Johnny left the message on Mike Murphy's mobile phone. Surely, he must have noticed the message by now, so why aren't the police here to rescue them. Johnny decides to ring again, but feeling in his pockets, his mobile phone is missing and gives a loud sigh of despair," Oh no, I must have dropped my mobile in the creek, when we jumped in, I won't be able to contact Danny and let him know we are safe for the time being." After slowly making their way up the muddy bank and onto a boardwalk at the rear of the bird hide in the Boondall Wetlands Park, they are both exhausted and decide to lay low for a while. Cherie looks a little brighter now, even though her hair is bedraggled, but maybe the quick dip in the water has freshened her up a little. She is shivering due to the air temperature being much colder now and she is still only wearing the clothes borrowed from Johnny's daughter. Johnny is still feeling some pain from his injured ankle and cut hands, but at least the bleeding has stopped, and the blood has been washed away. Seeing that Cherie is shivering from the cool night air after being soaked to the skin in the cold water, he takes off his wet jacket and wraps it around her hoping it may help to warm her up a little. It prompts her to look at him gratefully and give him a small kiss on his cheek saying, "You're my hero."

Chapter 27

MEANWHILE, BACK
AT THE CO-OP

Back at the co-op, the boss is on the deck looking up and down the creek trying to work out where Johnny and Cherie may have gone. Did they go right, or did they go left or did they go straight across and make it to the other side. He thinks he may have even injured or killed one of them by firing his pistol, which was probably a mistake, but reasons to himself that he will only need one of them alive to be able to find the missing contraband. The Santa Maria is now alongside the co-op dock and Tony has jumped across from the Santa Maria, securing it by a rope. The boss asks Tony, "What is over there?" pointing to the opposite bank of the creek.

Tony replies "Over there? It's The Boondall Reserve Wetlands, boss."

This means nothing to him so he asks impatiently, shaking with rage, "But can they escape that way?"

"Oh yes boss, there's a trail through the wetlands to an environmental shelter, which is near the Gateway motorway, they could easily get away, in fact they could even make their way across the Gateway to the Shorncliffe railway line at Boondall station and catch a train back here or even in the opposite direction that goes to the city.”

“Bollocks!” he shouts angrily. “Is there any entrance by road from the Gateway that will enable us to get into the wetlands and cut them off?” demands the boss.

“Oh yes boss, there is, do you want me to show you?”

“Yes, of course I bloody want you to show me, you fool,” he replies sarcastically, “Come with me and show me? Ronny, you take the Santa Maria and go up and down along this riverbank and use the searchlight to see if you can spot them on the other side. If you do, let me know straight away.” Ronny nods his agreement. “Tony, get in the car and come with me. Show me where the entrance to this bloody Boondall Wetlands is.”

Tony casts off the rope he has fastened to the trawler and walks reluctantly towards the door of the dock nervously looking back at his beloved Santa Maria. “You take good care of my boat Ronny? Don’t go up Nundah Creek will you, it’s too shallow.” Ronny doesn’t respond. “Do you hear?” Ronny just shrugs his shoulders, smirks to himself and gives Tony a tell someone who cares expression.

They are now both seated in the mini and the boss makes a phone call, saying, “They got away Mr. B…” hearing a loud response, he moves the earpiece away from his ear, then continues, “Yes, they managed to escape to the Boondall Wetlands by swimming across Cabbage Tree Creek… yes Mr. B, we’re on our way there now… yes Mr. B, I’ll report back to you again soon…” He closes his eyes briefly then puts his mobile back in his pocket and drives off down Sinbad Street towards Palm Avenue. When they arrive at the railway crossing, the warning lights are flashing requiring the car to be brought to a sudden stop, as a train is just leaving Shorncliffe Station, and the barrier is now halting their progress. “Fuck!” says the Boss, who is tempted to go around the barriers, “How long is it going to take us to get there?”

“Only about fifteen minutes boss,” replies Tony. The boss is not amused, he thinks about going around the barrier, but decides not to as the train goes hurtling past them. After the train has passed, they speed off and not another word is spoken between them until they reach their destination. Meanwhile, after steering the Santa Maria for a couple of hundred metres along Cabbage Tree Creek, Ronny manages to turn the trawler around. He manoeuvres it slowly adjacent to the creek bank near the co-op again, being careful not to get too close and at the same time managing to shine a spotlight into the mangroves on the Boondall Wetlands side as the trawler heads in the direction of the junction with Nundah Creek.

MANDY LENDS A HAND

While drama has been unfolding on the co-op dock, no one has noticed a bubbly curly-haired blond female wearing jeans and a black hooded sweatshirt. It's Danny's wife, Mandy, who is concealed in almost the same spot by a tree that Johnny was, when he was checking out the co-op building earlier in the evening. It's Mandy's turn to play her role in the plan devised between Johnny and Danny. After seeing the mini speed away, she rings her husband on her mobile and is troubled when she discovers that he's clinging to a pillar underneath Baxter's Jetty. She tells him that she'll go immediately and collect her car from the golf course car park and assures him that it will be now be perfectly safe for him to come out when she arrives at the jetty to pick him up. When she arrives at Baxter's Jetty car park, her husband is no longer under it, he pokes his head out from behind the toilet block, runs to the car and jumps in telling her to drive to Shorncliffe Railway Station. He assures her it will be safer for them there to update each other on why things haven't gone quite to plan. At the railway station car park, Mandy explains to Danny that during the distraction caused by him and Jack, Johnny and Cherie hadn't left through the co-op roller doors as planned so she couldn't aid their escape in her car. She adds that after the bald man arrived in the mini and entered the building, she saw them both jump into the creek and there was a muffled sound like a gunshot. She presumes that their good friends must have swum across to the other side of the creek to the safety of the Boondall Wetlands. On hearing this, Danny responds by saying, "If they've escaped, I can't understand why Johnny hasn't contacted me to let me know they are safe and another thing, why aren't the police here yet, Johnny said he had rung Sergeant Murphy and left a message."

Mandy takes in everything he has said, replying, "Maybe we should ring the police ourselves then?" and takes out her mobile.

"No wait," says Danny putting his hand on hers to prevent her from making the call, "This guy in the mini might be the police, we have to be very careful what we do now Mandy, because we don't want them to find out about our involvement and who knows what they might do to Johnny and Cherie to make sure this is all covered up."

So, for the time being they decide not to do anything, except drive down the Gateway to the Boondall Wetlands, and try and find Johnny and Mandy who must be hiding in there somewhere. Then they might be able to whisk their friends away to freedom and when they know everyone is safe, then get the police involved. They also hope in the meantime Johnny might be able to phone them and give an update on what is happening. As they drive out of the railway station car park a single bike light is heading directly towards them and unable to see out of the windscreen, Mandy is forced to bring her car to a halt. It's Jack on his E-scooter. Mandy sticks her head out of the window saying, "Jack, thank goodness you are okay, but why haven't you gone home already?"

Jack says breathlessly, "Well, after doing my shift at Shelleys, I usually go home on the train from Shorncliffe. It's allowed to take E-scooters on the train, but there are no trains at this time of night, I've missed the last one. Anyway, I wanted to stick around and see how everything turns out. This has been so much fun."

"Where do you live Jack," asks Danny looking anxious, as he and Mandy don't consider this as fun.

"Northgate," replies Jack, "We used to live in Shorncliffe, but after I finished my schooling at St. Pats, my parents moved and it's dead easy to get from Northgate to Shorncliffe on the train for work."

"Northgate?" replies Mandy "Oh, we thought you still lived in Shorncliffe." She weighs up what to do for a few seconds, "Put your E-scooter in the back of the car," Jack does so, takes off his helmet and hops into the back seat. Mandy adds, "It's important for us to go to the Boondall Wetlands first Jack, but we should be able to take you home afterwards."

Feeling slightly hurt, Jack says, "I am eighteen you know?" The Colby's glance at each shaking their heads and the vehicle speeds off. During their journey along the Gateway, the conversation revolves around their concern for their friends and what has happened so far this evening.

Chapter 29

CORNERED

Johnny and Cherie have been resting in the Bird Hide for about 10 minutes and are feeling content in the knowledge that the only way they can be followed is by someone swimming after them, which is highly unlikely. They are both weary from their exploits over the weekend and their efforts to escape. Cherie's head is still aching from the blow the boss gave her, and Johnny has a throbbing in his ankle; however, he is thankful his hands are not giving him as much pain as they had before. Peering through one of the narrow openings in the bird hide used by birdwatchers; our couple are intently keeping a look out, but not for birds. The Santa Maria is approaching the junction where Cabbage Tree Creek and Nundah Creeks meet. There is a spotlight shining a beam of light into the mangroves along the creek bank and our couple have convinced themselves the spotlight is probably too far away to be able to spot them. They also know that the trawler can't risk coming any closer, as Nundah Creek isn't deep enough for the Santa Maria to navigate.

Johnny asks Cherie a question about Declan, "You said that after Declan lost his job, he managed to get work on the trawlers, which trawler was it?"

"It was the Santa Maria, Johnny, why?"

"So, he worked for Tony?"

"Well, yes he did."

"I've been thinking about that, do you think that maybe Declan might have been mixed up in all this drug smuggling before he left Australia, and maybe he earned enough money to be able to afford to go back to Ireland."

"But he didn't go back to Ireland did he, not to Cork anyway, his cousin said so, remember?"

"Mmm, strange though isn't it, he works for Tony, he shoots through, then Tony hits on you, makes you think, doesn't it?"

"Makes you think what?" Cherie responds curiously. Then the trawler spotlight suddenly hits the Bird Hide, they were wrong, the beam of light is strong enough to reach them after all. They duck down as low as they can to avoid being seen. Unfortunately, they may have already been spotted as Ronny is concentrating the spotlight directly on the Bird Hide and he reaches inside his pocket for his mobile phone to make a call.

Rest time is over for them, they must get a move on and try to make it along the boardwalk to the entrance of the Boondall Wetlands Reserve shelter which they know is close to the Gateway Motorway. If they can make the Gateway, they are aware they might even be able to make it to the Boondall Railway Station and catch a train to Sandgate and notify Sergeant Murphy at the Sandgate Police Station. This also reminds them that there must be a good explanation as to why Sergeant Mike Murphy hasn't responded to their phone call yet. Crouching down trying to keep out of sight of the beam of light and avoid being spotted again, they exit from the rear of the bird hide which is being lit up by the trawler's spotlight. They must make their way along a boardwalk through the mangroves of the Boondall wetlands.

The boardwalk is shaped like a figure "S" with no sides, which means they need to be careful not to slip over the edge as they don't want to end up in the mangroves and injure themselves any more than they have already done so. They are both feeling very bruised, tired, sore and sorry for themselves as they trudge along in the darkness, but the full moon is helping them to see their way in the dark a little easier. After travelling about a hundred metres along the wooden boardwalk it comes to an end. They have arrived at a T-junction and come to a halt at a sandy-coloured dirt path to the right and the left of them. "Which way?" asks Johnny, "I haven't been here for years."

'Me neither," replies Cherie, "But I do recall this path is a sort of loop, so whichever path you take it probably leads back to the Boondall Wetlands Centre." She looks right then left and thinks for a moment, "From memory, I think that the left path may be the shorter route."

"Okay then, left it is," says Johnny and he carries on hobbling along the path with Cherie doing her best to support him.

Because of the path's sandy colour and the light emanating from the moon, they managed to find their way along it more easily than they did the boardwalk, only occasionally bumping into melaleuca trees that sometimes impede them. One thing that always gives them a surprise is the occasional screech of a fruit bat.

Chapter 30

HIDE AND SEEK

The green Mini Cooper is flying along the Gateway, way over the speed limit. When a siren can be heard, the boss curses under his breath and slows down to the speed limit of 100. He is relieved when he becomes aware that it is not a police car following him, but the siren of an ambulance heading in the opposite direction, so he promptly speeds up again. When they arrive at the entrance to the Boondall Wetlands Reserve, the boss drives right up to the padlocked gates and his mobile phone rings, with the screen indicating it is Ronny. The boss answers, "What is it, Ronny?"

Ronny advises him that he has spotted their prey at the bird hide and this news causes the boss to have a satisfying smirk on his face while nodding his head and saying, "Okay we should be able to find them now. Ronny, you stay where you are until I tell you otherwise and let me know if you spot them again." He hangs up.

"What's happening boss?" enquires Tony.

"Ronny thinks he's spotted them at a bird hide, do you know where that is?"

"Yes boss, it's opposite the boat ramp in Shorncliffe, there's a track between here and the bird hide, but because its dark, they could find a hiding place anywhere in between."

"Never mind that for now, let's just find a way into the wetlands, it looks like the gate is locked."

They each have a torch in hand and approach the padlocked gate at the entrance to the Boondall Wetlands Reserve. Without hesitation, the boss pulls out his beretta, attaches the silencer and fires two dull shots at the padlock shattering it into pieces and allowing them to open the gate. The boss parks his mini in the car park and they stride along a boardwalk and up some steps to the wetlands environmental building which is in darkness. After using their torches to make sure no one else is around they proceed at a brisk pace for another 50 metres along a track at the rear of the building and stop when they see the path has split into two directions. The boss is still holding the beretta in his right hand waving it in each direction saying, "So which path should we take Tony?"

"I'm not sure boss; they could be coming either way."

"What!" he says impatiently.

"Well boss, both of these track's lead to that bird hide, so it depends on which one they take."

"Okay you take the left one and I'll go right and if you see or hear anything shout as loud as you can or better still, just phone me, otherwise we meet at the bird hide, do you understand?"

"Yes, understood boss."

The boss stands there not moving as he watches Tony start off along the track to the left until he is out of sight, except for his torchlight shining ahead of him. After taking in his surroundings, the boss slowly begins traversing the winding sandy path to the right while shining his torch ahead of him. He occasionally directs his torch either side of the path into the bushland, as he reacts to animal noises and bird calls that are unnerving to him but he carries on walking, albeit at a slow pace.

Mandy, Danny and Jack arrive at the gate to the Boondall wetlands and notice that the green mini is parked there and the gates are wide open. Mandy decides that her car needs to be out of sight, so parks at the far end of the car park in some scrub, making sure it is well concealed. On inspecting the gate's padlock and chain, it is obvious a forced entry has been made. They approach the main building but decide they might be exposed to great danger. Especially as Jack is with them and don't venture any further into the wetlands, returning to their car.

Although Jack is disappointed about this decision, they resign themselves to staying hidden in the car to wait and see who might return to collect the mini.

Chapter 31

A PHYSICAL ENCOUNTER

Johnny and Cherie are making very slow progress along the sandy path and are thankful when they come across a bench, gratefully sitting down and taking a break to regather their strength. Cherie's head is still pounding but Johnny seems to be coping with his injured ankle much better and he is enjoying the comfort of the bench and being able to raise his injured ankle off the ground to ease the throbbing.

Cherie continues the conversation they were having before it was interrupted when the spotlight landed on the bird's hide. "Johnny before, when you said Declan worked on Tony's trawler, well do you think that Declan going away might have been because he fell out with Tony over the drug smuggling?"

"Could have been. Maybe Declan double crossed them, and he had to go into hiding. Maybe Tony started going out with you to find out where Declan was?"

"Oh, I see, not because he might have fancied me then!" retorts Cherie.

Johnny takes a deep breath, puts his arm around Cherie, looks into her eyes saying, "Of course he would have fancied you, who wouldn't?"

She gives a wry smile, "Okay, you're forgiven, but you're right, I never even considered before that Declan's disappearance might have been something to do with the trawlers. But now we've found out about the drug smuggling, it does seem to be a bit of a coincidence."

"So, you agree then, that he might have got involved with the smuggling in some way Cherie?"

Cherie thinks for a moment, "You know Johnny, no, I don't think Declan would have got involved in anything to do with drugs." Her face softens, "His mother had a big influence on him, okay yeh, he was a piss pot, but he did know the difference between right and wrong, he always attended church services every Sunday with his mother when he lived over in Ireland. When he decided to leave Cork and come to Australia, she gave him a gold St. Christopher medallion, beautiful it was. She'd bought it when she visited the Vatican in Rome on a holiday, even had it blessed by a priest in Ireland. She made him swear to her on his life that he would always obey the law and be a good trustworthy citizen in Australia, no matter how hard things might become. He always wore that St. Christopher round his neck, it is very special to him."

The conversation ceases abruptly as they suddenly react to a bright light shining through the trees on their left, someone is walking along the long winding sandy path coming from the direction of the wetlands centre. Their first thoughts are of joy and relief as they imagine they will now be rescued, but then they give each other a fearful look and without a word being spoken they know they must get off this sandy path and hide somewhere as one of their predators is about to pounce. They slide over the back of the bench, dropping down into the mangroves and crawling to a spot where they hope they are well enough hidden to not be seen.

A couple of minutes later a tall man in a black suit reaches the same bench, he's holding a torch in his left hand, shining it ahead of him and he has a gun in his right hand. He sits down with his back to them, places his gun down on the bench, turns off the torch and puts it down carefully on the bench as well. He then takes a mobile phone out of his pocket and keys in a number. They hear it ring, and it is answered, "Yes boss."

"I haven't arrived at the bird hide yet, how close are you?"

"Not far away boss, I'm alongside the creek opposite the old co-op fishing buildings at present but should be at the bird hide in a few minutes. Have you spotted anyone yet?"

"No nothing yet, let's hope that they are still at the bird hide, because if they are, there will be no escape for them."

"Let's hope they haven't made it back to the gateway," replies Tony, "Or we are stuffed."

The boss takes in what Tony has said and replies, "You're right Tony, they must not get back to the gateway, look I'm going back to the wetlands building now, just in case they have managed to find their way over there, you carry onto the bird hide check it out and then come back and meet me at the entrance, but come along this same pathway I am on, I'll be waiting for you."

"Okay boss," Tony hangs up.

Whilst this conversation is taking place, Cherie has seen the gun, which was placed on the bench, she pats Johnny on his shoulder and with a determined look on her face starts moving stealthily towards the bench. Johnny knows exactly what's on her mind and tries to stop her but he's too late, before he can react, Cherie has reached her objective and is poised to snatch the gun away from this evil menace. When the boss shifts in his seat making ready for another phone call, Cherie stops and ducks down almost under the bench. This time Ronny answers his call, "Yes boss."

"Ronny, do you still have a good view of the bird hide?"

"Yes boss."

"Good, then stay there and let me know straight away if you spot them, okay?"

'Okay boss will do."

After putting his phone away, the boss stands, stretches and has a big yawn. Cherie seizes her chance and makes a grab for the gun on the bench, but in the darkness, she mistakenly grabs the metal torch instead and knocks the gun onto the ground. Startled by her appearance, the boss lashes out at Cherie striking her with the back of his hand across her cheek and follows this up by grabbing her violently by the throat. He is squeezing hard and choking her, causing much pain. Seeing that Cherie has taken on more than she bargained for, Johnny manages to hobble onto the path and puts his arms around this fiend from behind in a bear hug, holding onto him as tightly as he can, causing the boss to lose his grip on Cherie's throat. The boss has his hand across her mouth now and she manages to bite into his fingers forcing him to release his grip altogether, but he strikes her with his other hand knocking her to the ground. Johnny is still holding onto the boss for dear life, but after a brief struggle the boss swings around and catches him on his temple with his elbow. This causes Johnny to also fall to the ground holding his head. The boss stands over Johnny and bends down slightly to strike him again, but Cherie jumps to her feet and hits the boss on the side of his head with the torch. She then kicks him in his nuts, making him fall onto his knees in agony shouting, "You bitch!" Cherie responds to this by standing over him shouting, "Fuck you," and kicks him in the nuts once again, but much harder this time. The boss is on the ground writhing in excruciating pain, which gives this female warrior great satisfaction.

Cherie helps Johnny to his feet and supports him as best she can as they both head back towards the bird hide in a sort of shuffling motion, much the same as a couple in a three-legged race. This has left the boss on the ground still holding his nuts and desperately crawling around on the ground, scratching at the earth looking for his gun, which has fallen under the bench.

Chapter 32

BACK TO THE BIRD HIDE

Johnny and Cherie are hurrying along as best they can, the adrenalin has kicked in now and Johnny's ankle doesn't seem to hurt him as much as it did before. Maybe that's because he is distracted by the pain in his temple, from the elbow he received from the boss. Johnny is feeling slightly dizzy from this blow, but he marvels at Cherie's bravery. Her taking another blow to the head doesn't seem to have slowed her down at all, just made her more determined. He knows in his heart that she is far braver than he is. Being a hero in a film is much easier than being one in real life. She is still clutching the torch that she grabbed off the bench and used as a weapon against their protagonist. She hasn't needed to turn the torch on yet as they seem to be getting along the sandy path quite well so far, by the light of the moon. Johnny asks her, "What did you have to confront him for, he was going to go back to the Boondall Wetlands building."

Cherie is peering at him, looking a little weird with her eyes screwed, saying, "I'm sick and bloody tired of being chased, beaten up, kidnapped, held hostage and shot at by these people, I'm not going to let them get away with this Johnny. If I'd managed to get that gun off him, this would be all over now. It's about time we let them know who they're dealing with."

"Oh yeah," replies Johnny, who is now so in awe of this wonder woman. "And who are they dealing with exactly Cherie?"

She is face to face with him now, "Why we are agents 86 and 99 of course! We're the good guy's Johnny, we're Control and they're the bad guys, they're KAOS."

"Okay then Cherie," Johnny is now thinking that Cherie might have had too many knocks to her head today. He puts his hands on either side of her face saying," Let's just calm down shall we and get out of here, but you do know that if we'd run in the other direction towards the Boondall Wetlands building, and not this way, we might have managed to get away by now." Cherie just looks at him in a confused state.

As they near the bird hide, a torch light is heading in their direction which makes them jump off to the side of the sandy path into the mangroves. They are lying almost prostate in the muddy water using any of the vegetation available to conceal themselves. It's Tony Pesaro who arrives shining his torch, and his phone begins to ring.

Chapter 33

ANOTHER NARROW ESCAPE

Tony has not long left the bird hide and his phone starts ringing, he answers, "Yes boss."

"Where are you?"

"I've just left the bird hide boss, there was no sign of them there and I'm heading back to the Boondall Wetlands Centre, like you told me to."

"Forget that Tony, they just jumped me and tried to get my gun, but they failed, they did manage to take my torch though. They must be heading straight towards you; can't you bloody see them?"

"No boss, they haven't come this way, they could have gone anywhere."

"Anywhere? Take a guess Tony and make it a good one."

"Well, I suppose they could be headed towards Nundah Creek, it's low tide now and they might be able to get over to Dinah Island, but probably not back to Shorncliffe. Anyway, Ronny is watching along Cabbage Tree Creek if they try and go that way, he should spot them."

"Could they have gone back along the path you came on?"

"Doubt it boss, I definitely would have seen or heard them."

"Okay Tony, wait for me there, I'll be with you very soon."

"Okay boss, will do."

Whilst this phone call is taking place, Johnny and Cherie are out of earshot as they have managed to crawl away from the path and are now well out of sight behind some mangrove trees. Then, after quietly discussing several alternatives, they decide that their best option is to head to Nundah Creek. It's only a short distance away, and when they get there, the intention is to wade across to Dinah Island and hopefully to safety.

Chapter 34

RONNY HAS NEWS

Tony is standing on the sandy path not far from the bird hide, when the boss arrives. The boss looks dishevelled, his right hand has a white handkerchief wrapped around it and there is blood oozing from his fingers through his makeshift bandage. The boss is angry, his suit is covered in dirt from being felled by Cherie, and his hand is throbbing from the deep teeth marks she managed to inflict on him, not to mention the pain he still has from being kicked twice in his testicles. He's had to stumble along in the dark, because this vixen has taken his torch from him.

"Still no sign of them Tony?" he scowls.

"No boss" says Tony noticing his bloody bandaged hand and untidy state of dress, which is a surprise to him as his boss usually looks immaculate in his Italian-made suits. "What the hell has happened to you then boss?"

"Never mind about that," he replies sharply, "Just tell me where they can be."

"Are you sure they came this way, boss?"

"Of course I'm bloody sure, you idiot…" his phone starts to ring, and he answers angrily, "Yes Ronny!"

"Boss, good news, I've spotted them."

"Where, back at Shorncliffe?"

"No boss, they were wading across Nundah Creek, heading towards Dinah Island, I just spotted them in the trawler's spotlight."

"Well, why didn't you go after them Ronny," he says sarcastically, "Go up Nundah Creek and get after them, you fool!"

Tony interrupts anxiously, "No, no boss, he can't take the Santa Maria into Nundah Creek, it's too shallow..."

"Alright, alright, Tony," he snaps back, "But if they are now over on Dinah Island, how the fuck are we going to get after them?" The boss gives Tony a piercing look, making him feel very uncomfortable.

Tony thinks for a few seconds, "We've got a tinny with an outboard motor back at the old co-op building boss, we could go and get it and use it to look for them, it can operate in shallow water, so there would be no problem."

"Why the fuck didn't you mention this before, moron." He talks into his phone again, "Did you get all that Ronny?"

"Yes boss."

"Okay Ronny, we're heading back to the co-op now, so bring the trawler back and meet us there, anyway it must look very suspicious you hanging around where you are," he hangs up and Tony looks relieved that his precious Santa Maria has not been damaged. "Come on Tony, let's get back to the car, we must stop them leaving Dinah Island, even if we don't get the drugs, we must finish them now or things will get really bad for all of us."

"How do you mean, boss?" replies Tony and they give each other a look, knowing exactly what this means.

They start walking back towards the Boondall Wetlands Centre entrance, but not as fast as Tony would have thought his boss would have liked. He notices his bandaged hand seems to be causing him pain and he is hobbling slightly. Tony decides not to mention the boss's state again as he doesn't want to inflame him anymore.

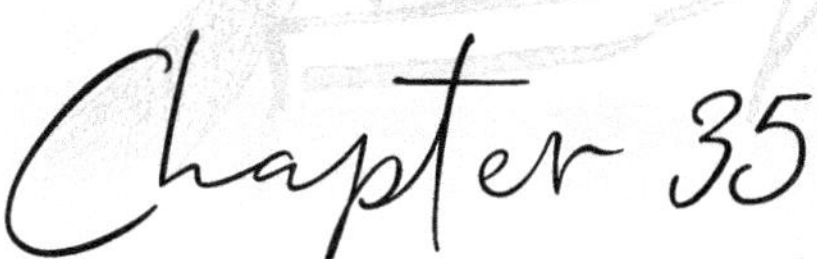

Chapter 35

TO THE CREEK

Johnny and Cherie have reached the bank of Nundah Creek and as it is low tide they will be able to wade across to Dinah Island and maybe make their way to the other side and retrieve Cherie's kayak and the contraband that they left high in a tree on Sunday morning. Johnny's head is still spinning from the blow he received from the boss's elbow, and he's concerned that Cherie may have a slight concussion from the blow to her head. She was acting strangely before, so he decides to check her out.

He puts his hands tenderly on her cheeks and looks lovingly into her beautiful blue eyes, "Are you okay Cherie?"

"Yes of course I am, what about you?"

"I feel a little dizzy to be honest, but I'll manage. But are you sure that you are okay Cherie, you were talking a bit strange before, you know, what you were saying, all that stuff about the good guys and the bad guys? And trying to get his gun off him, that was such a risky thing to do you know."

"Oh that, well I'm fed up with these guys pushing us around, and you must be too?" She now has her hands on Johnny's shoulders.

"Well yes but…" he hesitates.

Cherie is serious now, "But nothing Johnny, we've come this far, we are not going to let them win, okay?"

He smiles, "Okay agent 99," and rolls his eyes, "Wish I had a shoe phone though." Cherie doesn't understand what he is talking about as she has already forgotten the mention of Control and KAOS she made earlier but gives him a big kiss on his cheek anyway.

They hold hands and start traversing Nundah Creek, confident they should be able to cross to Dinah Island by wading up to their waist at most. Everything seems to be going fine, but when they are halfway across Johnny's head starts spinning again and he notices a swirling mist gathering around them and he can see an old-fashioned wooden boat in the distance, emerging from the mangroves on Dinah Island. The boat is heading directly towards them, aboard the craft sits an elegant lady wearing a headband and dressed in a long white dress. She is alone, her face is very pale, and she looks ill. It's Johnny's wife Sarah again, this time she's waving at him furtively, looking very concerned, he senses that she is trying to warn him of some danger. He glances at Cherie, but she doesn't seem to notice what he is seeing.

Just as the wooden boat is about to reach them, they are bathed in a large pool of light, which Cherie does react to. It's the spotlight from Santa Maria which is stationary in Cabbage Tree Creek. Ronny has spotted them and is shining the spotlight straight at them. The wooden boat is no longer visible to Johnny, so he shakes his head and pulling himself together, they urgently press on by continuing to wade across Nundah Creek. Wading across this creek is made difficult, due to the sticky mud threatening to suck off Johnny's trainers and Cherie's boat shoes. When they thankfully reach the muddy shore of Dinah Island, they urgently seek cover in the Mangroves. This means they are safely hidden as they can no longer be seen in the trawler's spotlight. They are wet and cold and sit down on the ground hugging each other in another attempt to keep warm.

Chapter 36

JACK OFFERS HIS SERVICES

Tony and the boss have finally made it back to the green mini cooper and don't notice Mandy, Danny and Jack crouched down in her car tucked away in the far part of the car park. The boss makes a quick phone call, "It's me Mr. B… no, we think that they are now on Dinah Island… alright we know that they are on Dinah Island… we are on our way to get a tinny. Yes, Mr. B, I'll let you have more information soon…" the person on the other end has obviously hung up. The boss gives a big sigh, revs up the mini and races off back up the Gateway Motorway towards Shorncliffe.

Mandy and Danny look at each other wondering what they should do now. Should they enter the Boondall Wetlands to see if any harm has come to their friends or should they set off in pursuit of the mini to see where it is off to? Before they can say anything, Jack's head pokes between them saying, "Do you want me to go into the wetlands on my E-scooter and see if I can find Johnny and his girlfriend?"

"What!" exclaim Danny and Mandy in unison.

"Yeah, it won't take me long on my scooter. I know this place, we came here on a school trip once, the pathway has a good flat surface, and the boardwalks are no problem for the bike either. I could just do the loop, check out the bird hide and come straight back, what do you say?"

Reasoning, any danger has just left the car park, the Colby's agree to this offer of Jack's services.

Jack steps aboard his E-scooter, puts on his dark blue helmet and begins spouting Shakespeare, "Parting is such sweet sorrow that I shall say goodnight till it be morrow."

"You get back here as quick as you can young man," insists Mandy.

As Jack is speeding off, he raises a clenched fist into the air and continues quoting the bard, "A man can die but once." And he is gone.

Danny is very concerned, "Shit! maybe it wasn't such a good idea getting him involved in all this Mandy?" She nods in agreement and looking equally worried as Danny she says, "I hope that boy's not going to be reckless."

Chapter 37

PROGRESS IS SLOW

Johnny is feeling particularly wary now as he knows this island is probably a sacred burial place for the Turrabul people. Aboriginal funeral traditions and ceremonies are deeply significant to Indigenous people as they strongly believe in the afterlife. But what alternative do they have, it seems to be the only escape route for them. He knows that white people have lived here in the past as there were reports of cattle being raised on this island in the nineteenth century. In the 1920's it's said a family called the Fergusons raised bananas, pineapples, watermelons and other fruits and vegetables here. An army map of that time shows two huts on the northern end of the island. And even in the 1960's people were still reported as living over here.

They are both really feeling the cold now and Cherie is still wearing Johnny's jacket. However, their dips in the water seem to have woken them up, brought them to their senses and shaken them out of their dizziness, tiredness, slight concussion, or whatever it was before that was making them behave either irrationally or illusionary. The reason was probably because they each received heavy blows to their heads, two for Cherie and one for Johnny. They continue onward undaunted into Dinah Island; Cherie still has her compass in her pocket and feels she may have to refer to it occasionally to make sure they are headed in the right direction. Johnny looks at his wristwatch, but it seems to have stopped much earlier that evening. Caused by climbing over fences, through windows and having watery encounters, but Johnny estimates that it must be well after midnight now. They head off in a northerly direction and hope that the kayak, paddles, life preservers and the contraband are all still where they left them, high up in a pandanus tree.

Although nature has reclaimed much of the land that Europeans would have cleared on Dinah Island in the nineteenth and twentieth century, the terrain is not as bad as Johnny would have thought. It is no wonder that they were able to raise cattle and grow certain fruits on the island back in the day. They proceed slowly but surely across the middle of the island, avoiding the marshy areas along Cabbage Tree Creek, as they do not want to be seen by their pursuers who might be searching for them on a certain trawler. Cherie only occasionally uses the torch she stole. Every now and then she turns it on to check her compass and make sure they are on the right course to where they left the kayak and the contraband.

Chapter 38

THE PRODIGAL JACK RETURNS

It has only taken Jack about ten minutes to circumnavigate the pathways from the Boondall Wetlands Centre to the bird hide and back on his E-scooter and when he returns, he can't wait to give his report to an anxious Danny and Mandy.

"Okay, no sign of Johnny and his girlfriend, in fact no sign of anyone, but I did notice a trawler out in Cabbage Tree Creek shining it's spotlight towards the banks of Dinah Island."

" That's excellent Jack, anything else?" asks Mandy.

"Well, yes there was something else that I noticed, you're not going to like it though."

Danny looks worried, "Just tell us Jack."

"Okay, there was this bench, not far from the bird hide and it looked like there had been a scuffle around it, but I don't think it was possums or anything like that."

"What do you think it was?" asks Mandy, closing her eyes.

Jack gulps, "Not too sure, but there was a lot of fresh blood on the bench, and I'm sure it wasn't any animal's blood. Sorry to be the bearer of bad news."

"Shit!" exclaims Danny, "They had better not have hurt them, but where can they be? Right, quick, let's all get back in the car, we're going back to Shorncliffe to find out what's going on."

"Sorry Jack," adds Mandy, "There isn't time to take you to Northgate now and we can't leave you here, so you will have to come back to Shorncliffe with us. Hope that your parents aren't worrying where you might be."

"That's fine" replies Jack gleefully, as he is really enjoying this adventure of a lifetime and adds, "Anyway they've gone away for the weekend, and won't be back till Monday." He's lying.

They leave the wetlands car park and travel up the Gateway Highway heading back to Shorncliffe as fast as they can.

Chapter 39

A GHOSTLY ENCOUNTER

Johnny and Cherie have reached the centre of Dinah Island, not that they are sure of their exact position on the island though. Johnny's ears prick up as he can hear the humming sound of a didgeridoo coming from a clump of paper bark trees and he is so relieved when he knows that Cherie has reacted to the sound as well.

"You can you hear that?" enquires Johnny.

"Yes of course I can, Johnny, I may have been knocked about a bit, but I'm not deaf."

"Sometimes, when the wind is in a certain direction, I can hear that sound coming from over here, but no one else seems be able to, it is a didgeridoo isn't it?"

Cherie looks puzzled, "Certainly sounds like one, but who could it be?"

They approach the clump of paper bark trees and in a small clearing beyond the trees they are surprised to see a ghostly look-ing figure, it's an Indigenous man sitting on the ground in front of a small fire playing a didgeridoo. He has grey hair and a grey beard and is only wearing a pair of Queensland Maroon's Rugby League shorts, and he is almost totally covered in white paint, which seems to illuminate him in the firelight. When Cherie shines the torch on him, he jumps up and grabs a spear that is lying by his side saying, "What are you white fellas doing here?"

Instantly recognising his friend Dudley Brown's voice, Johnny shouts back, "Dudley, is that you!? So, you're the one who's been playing a didgeridoo over here all this time?"

"Maybe," replies Dudley putting down his spear. "Hey, you two look like you've had a rough night, why are you over here?"

"Well, we have had a rough night," replies Johnny looking at himself and Cherie, whose clothes are dirty, torn and blood-stained, "But it wasn't our intention to come over here."

"What are you up to over here Dudley?" enquires Cherie.

"No offence Cherry…"

She interrupts him, "It's Cherie."

"Oh sorry, no offence my Cherie amour, but it's really none of your business what I'm doing over here, let's just say it's my culture, okay. But what I want to know is how did you manage to get over here, this is sacred land you know."

Johnny takes a deep breath, "Yes I do know, sorry Dudley, we don't mean to disrespect your customs, but we had no choice in coming over here, you see we are being hunted by some bad people who want to do us harm." Taking another deep breath, he continues, "You see, they kidnapped Cherie yesterday and kept her hostage in the old co-op fishing building, but I managed to free her last night. Then we managed to get away to the Boondall wetlands by swimming across Cabbage Tree Creek." He exhales, "They very nearly caught us over there, so coming here was our only option, it was the only way we could escape from them again."

Dudley has calmed down now, "Oh, that's not good news, you both look terrible," he pauses, "Look, let me welcome you to country," and they nod in acknowledgement, "So why are they after you, Johnny?"

"Good question Dudley," Johnny takes another deep breath, "We found out some people are smuggling drugs into Shorncliffe by using a trawler. We found a USB and from a code on it we worked out the location where the drop off place was. It ended up being contraband dropped from a ship, this all happened on Saturday night near Mud Island, but before their trawler could collect it, we snatched it."

"You snatched it?" laughs Dudley. "Really, how did you manage to do that, did you both swim out there?"

"Of course, not," replies Cherie shaking her head indignantly, "We paddled out there in a kayak."

"Wow, sounds like you've have had quite an adventure, so what's the plan now?"

"Well, it's not really a plan," shrugs Johnny, "But we are going to try and retrieve Cherie's kayak and the contraband that we hid on the edge of Dinah Island on Sunday morning."

"Oh really, and where abouts did you hide all that contraband?" enquires Dudley with a big grin on his face.

"Not far from here actually, we left everything on the North side of this island," replies Cherie looking at her compass.

"Yes," adds Johnny, "Can you help us to find it Dudley?"

"I don't have to," says Dudley looking pleased with himself.

"Oh really, and why don't you have to Dudley?" says Cherie looking slightly perturbed.

"Because Cherie, my dear, I've already found your Kayak and the big black bag, haven't I."

"You have!" says Johnny looking at Dudley surprised.

"Yes, I found it yesterday and moved it to a place where those bad fellas will never find it. Anyway, just as well I did move it, because the tides coming in now, and the water would have been much too deep for you to get to it again, well not until the tide has gone down, which won't be for a few hours yet.

"Really Dudley? And did you advise the police what you've found?"

"The police?" says Dudley laughing out loud, "No way Johnny, you know you can't trust the police."

"I'm inclined to agree with you there, Dudley," replies Cherie nodding her head, "But if you could just let us use your mobile phone, we need to advise some friends that we are okay."

"Mobile phone?" chuckles Dudley, "I don't do mobile phones when I'm on cultural business."

Cherie looks crestfallen, "Then, are you able to show us where you hid everything Dudley?" pleads Johnny.

"Of course I will mate, but it looks like you might need some rest first and I do have some water here," he picks up a canteen of water that was lying on the ground, "You look like you need a drink, would you like to have a drink?"

Johnny and Cherie don't need a second invitation and they both nod in agreement and sit down on the ground in front of the small fire, grateful to take a short rest and warm themselves. They take turns having a drink from the canteen until they are both fully sated. After which they embrace lovingly.

Chapter 40

MEANWHILE BACK AT SHORNCLIFFE

The green mini has sped back up the Gateway Motorway and after travelling along Bracken Ridge Road to Shorncliffe, it makes its way to the rear of the old co-op fishing building where Ronny has already moored the trawler. Tony has a tinny with an outboard motor stored in the building and the boss is getting very impatient because he considers it is taking Tony too long filling the outboard motor with fuel. He thought the aluminium craft would be ready as soon as they arrived. "Ronny, why couldn't you have got the tinny ready before we got here," snarls the boss to which Ronny just shrugged his shoulders. Then, all three of them carry the tinny to the edge of the creek and launch it onto the water. When they are all on board, Tony starts up the motor, takes the tiller and they head towards the mouth of the creek.

As the tinny leaves the co-op building, Danny, Mandy and Jack arrive in Sinbad Way and after seeing that the trawler is moored and there is no activity on board, Jack says, "When I saw this trawler it was much further up the creek and it was shining a spotlight onto the banks of Dinah Island." They decide to drive along a bit further making their way into Allpass Parade and spot a tinny skirting Dinah Island containing three men. Danny can make out that one of the men is bald and wearing a black suit, "That's the guy that Johnny described as the one he saw at the hospital and I'm sure he's the same person I saw at Unplugged Café on Friday night."

"Are you sure, Danny?" asks Mandy.

"Absolutely sure!" replies Danny.

"Wizzo!" exclaims Jack, poking his head between them with a big grin on his face, "Let's get him."

Danny and Mandy just look at each other and roll their eyes, both thinking that maybe it might have been a mistake to involve Jack in their escape plan tonight. Jack continues, "But how are we going to follow them now? We don't have a boat."

Mandy looks at Jack and then Danny, "No we don't Jack, but we do know someone who does!"

Chapter 41

A GRIM DISCOVERY

Cherie and Johnny feel refreshed after drinking from Dudley's canteen. They let him know they're ready to carry on to where he has concealed the kayak and the contraband and help him to put out the embers of the fire. Dudley is holding his didgeridoo in one hand and his spear in the other and says, "Okay, you love-birds, time for us to get going, I moved everything to the southeast part of Dinah Island, to a place where no one can find it, no one except me of course."

Cherie takes out her compass, looks at it and says, "Southeast did you say Dudley?"

"And you can put that away Cherry… sorry Cherie, I don't need a compass to find my way around sweetheart."

"How about a torch?" she asks holding it up, "Do you have any use for that?"

"Not yet," replies Dudley, "The moonlight will be sufficient for us to find our way for the time being."

Dudley leads the way, with Johnny and Cherie following close behind. After they have been trudging along for a few minutes through a particularly dense group of melaleucas, Dudley becomes increasingly aware that his followers are finding the terrain difficult to manage. If there were tracks once made by the people who lived here, they have been overgrown for a long time.

So, he turns around and assessing their condition says, "Let's go a different way, it might take a bit longer, but it will be a lot easier for you." They both nod with gratitude in agreement.

As they are passing a thick group of Pandamus trees, Dudley notices something on the ground and stoops down to pick it up, it's a dirty looking handkerchief screwed up in a ball. When he opens it out it, it reveals a monogram 'M. C-J' woven into it. "Now this is a very fancy handkerchief for someone to be using in the mangroves," remarks Dudley, "I wonder how this got here?"

"Can I see it please?" requests Cherie taking it tentatively from Dudley and then scrutinising it closely. "This looks like a very expensive handkerchief," states Cherie, "It's definitely a man's handkerchief, probably English linen I would say."

Johnny is also interested, he takes the handkerchief from Cherie and studies it, "There appears to be spots of blood on it, maybe we should have a search and see if there's anything else unusual around, you never know, maybe the smugglers have been here."

Dudley borrows Cherie's torch and enters the group of tangled Pandamus trees and returns after a couple of minutes looking stunned saying, "I've found something, or rather someone, partially buried, looks like the body's been here a while."

"Someone is buried here?" enquires Cherie, "But this is an indigenous burial site, isn't that to be expected?"

"Maybe," replies Dudley being defensive, "But I don't think this is one of my people, I think it's one of yours."

"Stay here Cherie," says Johnny stepping forward reluctantly and taking the torch off Dudley, "I'll go and have a look."

"No," says Cherie grabbing his arm firmly, "We'll go and look together," and side by side they enter the thicket interested to see for themselves what Dudley has found.

It's not long before they locate what Dudley has discovered. The remains of a grisly skeletal human are lodged in the roots of a Pandamus tree and the torchlight highlights mud crabs and other creatures crawling around in the gaps of the rib cage. Johnny almost gags, but Cherie remains calm and it's immediately obvious to both, that due to the state of the corpse, it's lain here for a few years.

Johnny comments, "I wonder if the handkerchief Dudley found might belong to this person… you said it was a man's handkerchief, didn't you?" Cherie nods in agreement. Johnny looks at the handkerchief again that he is still holding, "So, the initials 'M. C-J' suggests he had a double barrel name then," adds Johnny. "That should make it easier for him to be identified."

Johnny continues to shine the torch at the remains and Cherie is now peering intently at the rib cage as she can see something reflecting in the light created by the torch. It's very shiny and looks like something made of gold might be lodged in there. She recoils in horror, certain in the knowledge what she is seeing and lets out a heart-breaking cry, which is followed by her saying, "No, no, no, no, no," she falls to her knees sobbing uncontrollably. Johnny is trying to console her, not knowing what has caused her distress.

Dudley arrives, with his spear at the ready saying, "What is it, what's happened?"

"I don't know," says Johnny, still trying to console Cherie, as he continues shining the torch at the corpse, "What's the matter Cherie, what's upset you?"

Cherie is finding it hard to get her breath, she is sobbing unconsolably and pointing at the rib cage of the skeletal remains, but manages to blurt out, 'It's not his handkerchief."

"How can you be sure," says Dudley.

"Because this is Declan! It's my husband, he's wearing the St Christopher that his mother gave him, I'd know it anywhere."

"Oh my god!" says Johnny, who has now noticed the gold St. Christopher, and remembers Cherie telling him about how Declan's mother had given it to him. Johnny has continued to shine the torch at Declan's remains and has noticed what appears to be a small hole in Declan's skull but doesn't mention it to her. "So, I suppose the handkerchief might belong to whoever murdered Declan," Johnny doesn't know what else to say.

Cherie can hardly stand up now, she is distraught and can't stop shaking. Johnny carefully leads her out of the mangrove trees, whilst doing so he hands the torch to Dudley and indicates by tapping on his head that he wants him to go and have a closer look at the skull. Dudley crouches down and shines the torch to inspect the skull and after gently picking off a mud crab from the jaws he can see the hole that Johnny indicated to him. He is sure it is a bullet hole, so he sticks a finger and a thumb deep inside the open mouth of the skull and after a bit of groping around manages to latch onto a small metallic object and scoops out a bullet. When he re-joins Johnny who's still trying to console Cherie, Dudley manages to show him what he has found without Cherie knowing. Johnny discreetly takes the bullet off him and shoves it with the monogrammed handkerchief into his pocket, fully aware that this could be crucial evidence needed later.

Cherie suddenly stiffens and cries out, "How did Declan end up here?" And answering her own question, she says venomously, "It must have been because he was working on that trawler, those bastards killed him, because he wouldn't go along with all the illegal stuff they were involved with. Somebody with the initials 'M. C-J' was responsible for his death."

Chapter 42

HELP IS ON ITS WAY

Mandy has parked her car at the Sandgate Yacht Club and because it is the early hours of the morning, the three of them are being as quiet as they can creeping along the wooden walkways where leisure boats are moored. It doesn't take them long to find the yacht that they are looking for, a fifty-three-foot black-hulled beauty called the Acadian. Mandy and Danny have been here once before when the Boudreaux's hosted a closing night cast party for the theatre group, after one of their plays.

Danny can see that there is a light coming from a window of the Acadian, so they all climb aboard the yacht, and Danny gently taps on the cabin door. When the door opens Amelie is standing there looking very surprised in her dressing gown. She looks like she may have been expecting someone else at this late hour. Her husband Guy, also in a dressing gown arrives from another part of the yacht and can be heard saying, "Is he finally here Amelie?"

"No dear," she replies quickly, "It's our dear friends from SATS." and she ushers their visitors into the stateroom.

"My goodness," Guy responds, with a startled look on his face, "What on earth are you doing here at this time of night?"

"I'm sorry if we woke you," pipes up Mandy, "But we've come to ask for your help."

"Oh no, don't apologise, we often stay up late reading," replies Guy, "So, what kind of help do you require? It's a bit late for fund raising though."

"We need a boat," adds Jack bluntly.

"You need a boat, at this time of night?" Guy sounds intrigued, "What for?"

"We need you to help us rescue our friends," Danny tells them in a serious tone.

"Well sit down all of you, let's talk about this," says Amelie calmly, and asks, "Would you like a cup of coffee? You all look very tired."

They agree to a cup of coffee, except Jack who has a bottle of soft drink. Danny proceeds to tell them that he thought Johnny was acting strange when he phoned him on Sunday, but afterwards Johnny confided in him that he and Cherie had found some drugs whilst kayaking near Mud Island on Saturday night, resulting in Cherie being kidnapped and held hostage and they'd devised a plan to rescue her, but that it had not gone quite the way they expected. He tells them, Mandy saw Johnny help Cherie escape to the Boondall wetlands and after that they believe they had managed to get to Dinah Island as the three men who were at first looking for them using a trawler, were now searching for them by skirting Dinah Island in a tinny and it won't be long before they might do some harm to their friends.

Guy and Amelie are listening intently to Danny's thorough report and when he finishes Guy responds by saying, "And why haven't you gone to the police to tell them about all this?"

"No, we can't, because we think the police might be involved and if we did, they might just kill the both of them to cover all this smuggling up," says Mandy."

"Is this all to do with the USB that Johnny told us about on Friday night the one he found in the hollowed-out log in the woods?" asks Amelie, who gets a strange look from her husband.

"Yes, yes that's what started all of this" says Danny urgently.

Jack, who has grown very impatient while the others have been talking, stands up to join in the conversation saying boldly, "Look, we are wasting time, are you going to let us borrow your boat, or not?"

Mandy and Danny seem a little embarrassed by Jacks' outburst. Then Guy looks at his wife, who nods back at him in agreement, and then looks at Jack, smiles in a grandfatherly kind of way and replies, "Yes, of course you can borrow our yacht young man, but it may take us a little time to get the Acadian ready to sail."

Jack is rubbing his hands with glee, "You bloody beauty!"

They all react to him.

Chapter 43

RUB A DUB DUB, THREE MEN IN A TUB

Our three villains have been skirting Cabbage Tree Creek in the tinny while sometimes shining their torches into the mangroves when they hear any noise. Ronny is the one delegated to go ashore and have a quick search for the source of the sound, which always turns out to be some kind of local wildlife. They began searching in the tinny by the junction at Nundah Creek and have now worked their way around to just past the mouth of Cabbage Tree Creek, which ironically is very close to where Johnny and Cherie originally left the kayak and the contraband. Tony is manoeuvring the tinny close enough to the mangroves so that the boss can send Ronny ashore to scout around to search for any sign of their escapees. And although Ronny is not too thrilled that he is always the one having to go ashore and do the searching, he holds his tongue as he doesn't want to antagonise his boss who is in no state to do it and Tony is needed on the tiller of the tinny.

The boss is furious, "They must be in here somewhere, is there anywhere else that they could have gone," he demands to know.

Tony suggests, "The only place that they might be heading for is Nudgee Beach, you can walk over to there from here at low tide, but as the tide is coming in now, I don't think that they can make it from here, even if they are very good swimmers. They will need to go to the southeast of Dinah Island and attempt to swim the much shorter distance across an estuary to Nudgee Beach and freedom."

"Oh really," replies the boss, "Well, I happen to know that Johnny Blakemore is a very good swimmer, he regularly goes to the Sandgate Pool."

Tony is surprised at this revelation. "How do know that boss?"

He replies quickly and arrogantly, "Because a little birdie told me."

"Oh, I suppose that's one of your cop friends?" chimes in Ronny.

"You just shut the fuck up Ronny! That is nothing to do with you. Understand?"

Ronny backs off, "Yes boss, sorry boss, understood."

"Anyway," says Tony, "They wouldn't have had enough time to get across Dinah Island and to safety yet. And I doubt if Johnny Blakemore would try to swim across on his own and leave the woman behind. I think they are still in there, somewhere."

"So do I Tony," agrees the boss "And when we catch them, they are going to be very sorry, very sorry indeed."

The lights on the tall cranes at the Port of Brisbane can be seen clearly. The wind has picked up now, Tony was correct, the tide is starting to come in fast and the water is getting very choppy with the waves creating whitecaps that are visible in the moonlight.

Ronny is once again ordered to go ashore and have a scout round for any sign of their prey, which he does begrudgingly. This time though, he reaches a spot not far inside the mangroves and can see that some branches about two metres above the ground have been recently broken. It's not hard for him to work out that someone has been here. This is confirmed when he finds a black cap in good condition on a lower branch with the letters SATS embroidered in gold thread. On closer inspection the initials 'C. O'B' are marked on the inside of the cap. He shouts out, "Hey I found something!" triumphantly holding up the baseball style cap, "I reckon they've been here; they must have been here."

When Ronny rejoins them in the tinny, he reports that the mangroves seem to have been disturbed at the site and it looks like something might have been hidden there, but all he could find was the cap. After inspecting the cap, Tony advises the other two that the initials on the cap stand for the Sandcliffe Amateur Theatre Society and it must belong to Cherie O'Bryan as the initials inside, 'C. O'B' are hers. So, they all agree that the contraband must have been hidden there because they know that Cherie wasn't wearing a cap when they kidnapped her, so she must have lost it here on Saturday night when the contraband went missing. The boss decides they've wasted enough time searching for them along this stretch of water and orders Tony to head straight for the estuary near Nudgee Beach, certain that the runaways will try to cross there over to the township.

Meanwhile, the Acadian, a stunning, black-hulled Custom Motor Sailer yacht can be made out in the distance. Its sails are showing up against the lights along Allpass Parade, as it heads down the channel towards the mouth of Cabbage Tree Creek on its way out to sea. There is a maple leaf flag on its stern flapping in the breeze and a small inflatable rubber boat is being towed behind. On board, the yacht are the Boudreaux's, the Colby's and Jack Hollis, who is very interested in this stunning 34-metre beauty. Danny and Mandy seem anxious as they sit on deck chatting with Amelie who is currently steering the yacht out into Moreton Bay. In the meantime, Guy has been taking Jack for a tour around the yacht. Apart from showing him all the luxuries that the Acadian has to offer, he is telling him stories of some of the hair-raising thrills they encountered when they were on the high seas crossing the Pacific Ocean. He also lets him know how on each Good Friday they enter the Acadian into the Brisbane to Gladstone Yacht Race. Proudly telling him of the successes they have had and how they require extra crew members to do that event. All this fascinates Jack who has loaned the use of Guy's binoculars. He has been scrutinising the Dinah Island shoreline, although it is a bit gloomy at present to see anything clearly. He's also been shown some of the various navigation devices on board and other items needed in case the yacht was in distress.

A VOW OF RETRIBUTION

Johnny has managed to calm Cherie down somewhat, but she is still shaking and going over and over in her mind what might have happened to Declan for him to have ended up on Dinah Island. She had always thought he had run out on her a few years before, after the marriage had broken down due to their daughter Marie's cot death. And she now remembers all those times she had cursed him for leaving her. Thinking that he must have been having such a good time having a drink in a bar in Cork or in a Beer Keller in Munich or some other European destination. But no, he was lying here dead all that time, rotting away on Dinah Island, just a few kilometres from their home in Shorncliffe. She has become aware of how concerned Johnny is looking at her, and she tries to pull herself together and raise a smile. He's had his arm around her all this time trying to console her. She has grown strong feelings for Johnny over this weekend, not lust but genuine feelings. She is sure he feels the same way about her and hopes that if anything good should come of this, it will be that they could end up together. But before that happens, she knows that she can't let these people get away with murdering Declan and asks Johnny softly, "Do you have any idea how Declan was killed?"

Johnny thinks for a moment, as he is not sure how she will react to the truth, then he looks at Dudley who is standing quite close, who gives him a nod. Knowing he can't keep the truth from her any longer, he responds to her question, "Somebody shot him Cherie… in the head."

Cherie closes her eyes, taking it all in and Johnny is apprehensive about how she will react, but she doesn't scream this time, as she did when she saw Declan's gold St. Christopher, but merely exhales saying, "Oh, poor Declan," and with a controlled inner rage very slowly and very deliberately utters, "Okay, but when we do find out which one of these bastards killed him, I want my revenge, I want to end his life, is that understood?"

Johnny and Dudley look at each other, then Johnny turns back to Cherie in admiration, thinking this woman has more balls than he does, "I understand how you must feel Cherie, but these people are dangerous. They've killed Manny and may have killed Declan, but there's no way I want to lose you now after all that we have been through in the last couple of days."

"I know, I know," replies Cherie, touching his face, "And I don't want to lose you either, but I know what I must do." There is a deathly silence as they all come to terms with what she is contemplating. Cherie looks deeply into Johnny's eyes saying, "I want you do something for me Johnny, will you do something for me?"

"Err… yes anything Cherie," he stutters, but maybe not help you kill someone he is thinking, "Just ask?"

"Could you go and get Declan's St. Christopher for me please?"

"Err, yes of course I will," he says, so thankful that she doesn't want him to kill someone for her after all.

"I have already taken the liberty, my dear," pipes up Dudley, who had slipped away a few minutes before and retrieved the medallion from Dudley's remains whilst Johnny had been consoling her. "I hope I have done the right thing."

He hands it to Cherie who inspects it and then places it around her neck saying satisfyingly, "Yes you have, thank you Dudley."

"You are most welcome Cherry… sorry, Cherie, but I think we've spent enough time here, we should carry on and retrieve your kayak, and don't worry, I will let the authorities know exactly where they can find Declan after this is all over and then you will then be able to lay him to rest."

"Thank you, Dudley. Declan has been here so long with your people; I suppose being here a little bit longer isn't going to hurt him."

Dudley takes up his spear and didgeridoo and stands proudly saying, "Let's get a move on then," and starts walking off in a south-easterly direction with the others following him arm in arm not far behind. Cherie can't resist having a quick look at her compass to satisfy herself that they are going in a south-east direction.

Chapter 45

A NEW DAWN IS NIGH

Our three felons in the tinny are now arriving at the estuary near Nudgee Beach and the sky is beginning to get a little lighter. The rays of the sun have not yet begun to appear behind a few dark clouds on the horizon, but dawn is only about an hour away. It has been made more difficult getting here due to the rough sea but using Tony's experience in all types of boats they have made it safe and sound. Except for the boss that is, who doesn't seem to have as good sea legs as the other two. He has needed to throw up over the side of the tinny a couple of times already, making his expensive suit even more of a mess than it was before. He is worried that he will not be able to catch his prey and even more concerned that he'll not retrieve the expensive cargo that was stolen from right under the noses of his trawler crew. He has spoken several times to a mysterious man during the evening, each time giving him bad news. He knows that if he doesn't resolve this matter to this person's satisfaction, his head will roll, just as others have rolled before him. "How much longer before we get there?" he demands, looking a bit green around the gills.

"We've already arrived boss," Tony replies, in a matter-of-fact manner, "We just need to go ashore and wait until they arrive and when they do we should have them, because they won't be able to swim across this estuary to Nudgee Beach without us spotting them, and it's a hell of a walk back to Shorncliffe."

"Then let's get ashore now, so we can stop them. Let's secure the boat and take cover somewhere," orders the boss, eager to get onto dry land due to his motion sickness.

"Good plan boss," agrees Ronny, trying to suck up to him.

Once ashore Tony secures the tinny under some, She-oaks and the boss, who is relieved to be on dry land takes a deep breath saying, "Let's try and find a good hiding place for us, so we can take them by surprise when they get here."

They search around the mangroves trying to find an ideal spot to make sure they will not be seen by Johnny and Cherie when they get here. The boss receives a surprise phone call from Mr. B, which he tries to answer quickly, but only manages to fumble with his phone before saying, "Yes Mr. B… you're where? … and you're with who?" The others look at the boss who has an incredulous look on his face. "How did that happen?... oh really?" There is a long pause as the boss listens to what Mr. B is saying. He then replies, "We are at an estuary between Dinah Island and Nudgee Beach… oh, you know it? So, you're going to bring them here in a dinghy? Okay then Mr. B, we'll be ready when you get here." The caller hangs up.

The boss is now in a very agitated state, he tells Tony and Ronny to gather around and explains to them that there has been a slight change of plans because there is going to be a very important visitor arriving soon. There's a very important person arriving with a couple of people, who think they are going to rescue the ones already at large on the island. So, he needs them to be ready when they arrive, but they still need to stay alert and on the lookout for Johnny Blakemore and his girlfriend, as they are expected to arrive here very soon.

Chapter 46

DIVIDE AND CONQUER

The Acadian has sailed out into Moreton Bay and has anchored a couple of kilometres off the coast, directly in line with the estuary between Dinah Island and Nudgee Beach. All five on board are seated in the yacht's salon and Guy is explaining how they should approach this further. "So, because it is getting lighter now, and Jack's used my binoculars to confirm he's spotted three men in a tinny over there on Dinah Island. I need to ask, are you positive that they are not just some innocent fishermen?"

"No way," says Mandy, "They are the same men who were at the co-op building last night, that's where Cherie was being held hostage and Johnny managed to help her escape to the Boondall Wetlands."

"We also saw two of them up fairly close at the Wetlands Centre," agrees Danny.

"And I clearly saw the other one steering a trawler along Cabbage Tree Creek and shining a spotlight onto the banks of Dinah Island," adds Jack.

"Okay," says Amelie, "So why are you insisting that you don't want the police involved?"

Guy looks at his wife Amelie and says firmly, "No Amelie it's too late to involve the police now." Then he turns to the other three saying in a reluctant way, "Okay then, it seems that you are not going to be dissuaded from your task, but our yacht cannot go too close to shore because of the shallow water. However, we do have a dinghy in tow, so why don't four of us go ashore in the dinghy and have a chat with these guys. And Amelie, you can stay here with the Acadian."

Mandy looks concerned, "Oh, I don't think it's a good idea for Jack to come with us Guy."

"I'll be alright," insists Jack.

"Mandy is right Guy, let the boy stay here with me," insists Amelie looking at Mandy who is nodding in agreement.

"Very well Amelie," Guy sighs, "You look after Jack and the rest of us will go ashore in the dinghy."

"But…" says Jack.

"No buts about it Jack," interrupts Danny wagging his finger at him.

"Ohhhh, pooh, not fair," Jack is so disappointed.

Standing on the deck of the Acadian, Danny and Mandy don orange life preservers under Amelie's supervision, while Guy is making a quick phone call. Guy then dons his own life preserver and pulls the dinghy into place alongside the yacht and ascends into it, sitting at the rear. He is carefully followed by Mandy and Danny, who sit on either side of the small rubber craft. Guy starts the outboard motor, waves to his wife and away they go off to Dinah Island.

Jack feels let down as he watches the dinghy until it is just a speck in the distance. He then goes below deck to join Amelie, who is already standing by a dining room chair, and she is wearing an apron, "Can you please sit down here Jack," she requests politely.

"Oh, no thank you," he replies, "But Amelie, would it be possible for me to borrow Guy's binoculars again please? I want to go back on deck and try and find out what's happening on Dinah Island?"

Amelie pulls a revolver from her apron pocket and makes a further request, but this time in a sinister tone, "I said sit down Jack!"

He can't believe what's happening, why is she doing this. He reluctantly obeys her, whilst trying to understand what's going on. Amelie stands behind the dining chair pointing the revolver at Jack's head and gives him a stern order, "Put your hands behind your back," which he does promptly. She then secures his wrists together at the back of the chair, using large cable ties that she has also obtained from her apron pocket. She then uses a couple of more cable ties to secure his feet together, while always keeping her weapon pointed directly at him.

Jack's mind is working overtime, what is happening, are Guy and Amelie a part of this subterfuge as well. But how can that be, they are upstanding members of the community, being regular attendees to SATS plays and contributing generously to the theatre's fund-raising events. They are the last sort of people anyone would have thought could be linked with all this. He is starting to become worried about his friends, what is going to happen to Danny and Mandy when they reach Dinah Island, and what has happened to Johnny and Cherie, but also what is going to happen to himself. Maybe this witch as he now views her, plans to feed him to the sharks. He knows he must try and come up with some way of overpowering this woman so he can warn his friends they are in grave danger. "You won't get away with this you witch," he says defiantly, while struggling to break his bindings.

"Oh, wont I?" she replies sitting down on a sofa and pointing the revolver at him, "And how are you going to stop us then?"

He fixes her square in the eyes with a stare and angrily quotes the first Shakespearean lines that come into his head, "Double double, toil and trouble, fire burn and cauldron bubble."

Amelie walks up to Jack and slaps him hard across his face, causing his head to jolt back.

Jack sits up as straight as he can as a trickle of blood emerges from the corner of his mouth and he says defiantly and sarcastically, "Oh, not a fan of Shakespeare then?"

Amelie slaps him again.

Not to be outdone, he says, "Do your worst witch, I'm made of sterner stuff." She leaves the salon and goes up on deck.

Chapter 47

A CHANCE TO GET AWAY

Dawn is beginning to break and Dudley, whose white paint is less prominent now is still leading the way to where he's moved the kayak, paddles, life preservers and what this has all been about the drugs. "Is it much further, Dudley," implores Cherie, who is still coming to terms with finding her husband Declan's grisly remains. She is so tired now, her only recent opportunity to sleep was when she was tied up on the concrete floor at the co-op building, but does passing out count? She hasn't slept in her bed since Saturday night and that was only for about two or three hours.

"Not much further now Cherie, then I will be able to get you both safely away from here," Dudley says in a soft voice. He has gained so much respect for this lady, after hearing how she stood up to her kidnappers, oh yes, she is a real trooper in his eyes.

Johnny never knew that Cherie had so much about her, he can imagine her as the hero in an action-packed movie, "Wonder Woman," or "Harley Quinn" or maybe "Black Widow." He is very much aware that this is the lady he wants to be with after this is all over, if they should manage to survive that is.

"We're arrived," shouts Dudley who has disappeared behind a clump of wattle trees. They follow and lo and behold hidden in a mass of bungwall ferns there's the kayak, the paddles, their yellow life preservers, the large plastic bag containing the drugs, plus a sixteen-foot khaki coloured, Canadian Canoe.

"Wow Dudley, that's a nice canoe, where did you get that from?" asks an impressed Cherie.

"BCF," he says laughing and then stops, saying more seriously," Why, do you think I stole it?"

"I wouldn't care if you did," says Cherie admiring the canoe.

"We can paddle across the estuary and down the inlet to the rear of my place at Nudgee Beach," replies Dudley, "I live right on the inlet," he says proudly. "The canoe should be large enough to take us all, even your kayak should fit in, if we separate the two sections. But we will have to tow the plastic bag and its contents."

"You live at Nudgee Beach?" asks Cherie, seeking confirmation.

"Yes, Lima Street, my house backs right onto the wetlands canoe trail," Dudley confirms.

"Sounds good," says Johnny, eager to get going.

When the canoe is put onto the water and loaded up, Dudley becomes hesitant about towing the large plastic bag, so he persuades the others to leave it behind hidden in the bungwall ferns. They all agree that the most important thing now is for them to get away and worry about the contraband later, after they are home free. They take up their positions in the canoe, Dudley has his paddle and Johnny and Cherie don't bother putting on the life preservers and using their kayak paddles they slowly begin heading East across to the inlet.

They haven't been paddling for very long before there's a loud shout coming from the shore on Dinah Island, "There they are!" they have been spotted.

Chapter 48

SPOTTED!

The three felons are well concealed with the tinny in the mangroves as they wait for the arrival of Guy Boudreaux in a dinghy. The boss's mobile rings, and he reluctantly answers it, "Why are you ringing me, I told you to stay out of it?" He listens to what the caller has to say and responds by saying, "Well if you must know, we are waiting for the two of them to arrive so we can surprise them. And now we are expecting two more busy bodies, who went to the marina to ask for the use of a certain yacht." He listens again, "Yes that's right, they fell right into their laps, so it won't be long before we are rid of all of them, Okay? Now don't call me again, just make sure that as we agreed none of your people get involved, we will take care of everything." He hangs up.

It hasn't taken Guy very long to arrive at the rendezvous spot after leaving the Acadian and the three felons come out of hiding and out in the open to meet the dinghy at the water's edge. Guy asks Danny and Mandy to alight from the rubber craft and tells them to go ashore saying he will secure the dinghy. He does so but leaves the outboard motor ticking over as he wants to return to the Acadian as quickly as possible. As soon as his passengers' step onto dry land they see that there are three men there and one of them, with a bald head, wearing a rather messy suit is pointing a gun at them saying, "Welcome to Dinah Island."

When Guy joins them, he is also brandishing a gun, Danny and Mandy think there is going to be a standoff, but to their dismay, Guy also turns his weapon on them and orders them to hand over their mobiles to him, which they do. They also take off their life preservers when ordered to do so and drop them to the ground. "They came to us for help," Guy is chuckling, "They just fell right into our hands." Changing his tone, he says, "Now I want you to get rid of them, I'm going back to the Acadian."

Just then Ronny shouts out, "There they are!" he's pointing towards the estuary and everyone turns to look. There's a large Canadian canoe beginning to cross the estuary towards Nudgee Beach and on board they can see Johnny, Cherie and an indigenous man with a few white streaks of paint on his body, and they are all paddling furiously.

Whilst everyone's attention is drawn to the sighting of the canoe, Danny and Mandy take the opportunity to literally run for their lives into the mangroves.

The boss says, "Mr. B, we have to use your dinghy to stop the canoe from getting away," he points to where the tinny is hidden, "We don't have time to get the tinny ready, your dinghy's outboard motor is still running, they might get away if we don't get after them straight away."

"Very well," agrees Guy reluctantly, handing him the orange life preservers, "But be quick, you go with Tony and stop them and you Ronny, take my gun, go and find the other two and just finish them off, okay."

"Pleasure sir," replies Ronny, not really knowing who this man is, or exactly what he should call him, but sure that he is someone much higher up the food chain than himself. Then Ronny runs into the mangroves eager to impress by locating where the couple may have hidden themselves so he can finish them off.

Tony wades out to the dinghy and takes the tiller. When the boss is also seated and they have both put on their orange life preservers, he revs up the outboard motor and begins in pursuit of the three paddlers in the canoe. It doesn't take very long for the dinghy to catch up and draw alongside the canoe, whereupon the boss stands with a pistol in hand, trying to aim at Johnny. He manages to fire off a shot, just missing his target. At the same time as he fires the shot a spear thuds into the boss's shoulder piercing his life preserver and causing him to cry out in pain. "What the fuck!" and he drops his gun into the estuary. Dudley who had temporarily ceased paddling picked up his spear and expertly stopped the boss from inflicting any damage on them.

Not sure what to do now, Tony uses the dinghy to ram the canoe, which causes not only Johnny and Cherie to fall overboard on opposite sides, but also the boss still with the spear lodged in his shoulder, who tumbles awkwardly from the tinny into the estuary as well.

On witnessing everything that has happened, Guy locates the hidden tinny and drags it to the water's edge, deciding it's time for him to get out of there, Guy boards the tinny, but is having trouble starting up the outboard motor and the aluminium craft begins to slowly drift out into Moreton Bay. There are a couple of oars on board, so he gives up on motor power, secures the oars to the fitted oarlocks and starts rowing back to the Acadian when his mobile phone begins to ring.

Chapter 49

A KIND OF REDEMPTION

Sergeant Mike Murphy is sitting at his desk at Sandgate Police Station and has just finished a call on his mobile phone. He begins to again listen to the message that Johnny left him much earlier, "Hey Spud, it's Blakey mate, need your help urgently…."

He places his head in his hands and is startled when young P.C. Peter Wilson enters his office saying, "I'm just off home now sarge," and noticing his superior's sorry state adds, "Oh are you alright sergeant?"

"Yes, perfectly alright thank you Constable Wilson," he replies, quickly turning off his mobile and regaining his composure.

"Geez, you're working late tonight sarge, got a lot on your plate, have you?"

"Yeah, just have a lot of paperwork to catch up on constable, you know how it is, you get along now."

The P.C. goes to leave then hesitates at the door, saying with a consoling smile, "Oh well, don't overdo it sarge, there's always tomorrow, you know."

Sergeant Murphy refers to his wristwatch and tapping it says, "It's already tomorrow constable, that's the problem, running out of time."

"Oh," says the P.C. not quite understanding what his sergeant means, "Oh well, I'll be off then. Quiet night tonight wasn't it sarge? Nothing much exciting ever happens around here, does it? Good morning sarge."

"Good morning, constable," and P.C. Wilson leaves the room while Sergeant Murphy reflects on when he was a young police constable himself, just starting out in the police force and how he had so many morals back then. He suddenly stands and says to himself, "This has gone too far," then hurries to the office door and shouts down the corridor, "Constable Wilson, could you come back here please?"

There is the sound of footsteps coming back down the long corridor and on arriving, the P.C. puts his head around the door saying, "Yes sarge, is everything okay?"

"Yes, constable perfectly okay, but I don't want you to go home yet, I need you to help me put something right."

"Put something right sarge, how do you mean?"

"You'll find out soon enough constable, I just need to make a phone call first." He picks up the receiver of his desk phone, dials a number and when he gets an answer he says, "Water Police? Sergeant Michael Murphy here from Sandgate Police Station, I need your assistance urgently." The P.C. is still standing at the door wondering what is going on.

Chapter 50

MEANWHILE BACK ON THE ACADIAN

Back on the Acadian, Amelie is on deck looking through the binoculars towards Dinah Island, she wants to make sure that Guy has handed Danny and Mandy over to their miscreants. Down below in the salon, Jack has a large red mark on his left cheek showing the outline of Amelie's right hand from when she twice violently slapped him. He's still sitting in a dining chair restrained by large cable ties to his hands behind the back of the chair and to his feet.

He has been working out a plan of escape and remembers when they all had coffee earlier, he'd requested a bottle of soft drink instead, and that Amelie opened it for him using a barman's friend. He is now thinking that if he can get his hands on that bar tool, then he should be able to use the blade to cut the cable ties. But first, he must try and free his arms from the rear of this chair. He rationalises, that he needs to stand on the chair to enable him to raise his arms. Jack is a very lithe young man with a flexible body, in fact he was always considered an excellent dancer and once won a limbo competition at a friend's birthday party. So, with great effort and a lot of strength, Jack eases his way up the chair and manages to rest his feet where he is sitting. Once he is standing up, he is then able to raise his arms until they have cleared the backrest of the chair, but as he jumps off, he falls to the ground knocking the chair over. After getting to his feet and assuring himself that Amelie hasn't heard the noise he made falling, he manages to hop to a draw next to a sink where he hopes the barman's friend is located. With his back to the drawer, he pulls it open slightly and thankfully the bar tool is there. After trying a few unsuccessful positions, he works out that by lying on his back, passing his hands under his posterior and bringing his feet close to his hands he can open out the blade and with some considerable effort cut through the cable ties securing his ankles together. On hearing footsteps on the yacht's deck, he hurriedly gets to his feet, puts the broken cable ties and the barman's friend into his jean's pocket, picks up the chair and arranges himself back on it looking as he did before, still firmly secured.

Amelie steps into the room muttering to herself, she is not happy, something seems to have gone wrong. She locates her mobile phone and makes a call to her husband and when he answers she says hurriedly, "Guy, what's happened, why aren't you in the dinghy?... you're coming back in an aluminium boat... you're rowing it back... why?... because the motor won't start... alright, I will lookout for you... Are you sure they won't phone the police? ... oh, you have their phones? Well get rid of them now, throw them overboard." After the phone call Amelie walks behind Jack's chair and checks that the cable ties are still intact around his wrists, but to Jack's relief she doesn't bother looking at his ankles. Then she hurries back up the stairs and back on deck.

Jack gives a sigh of relief and promptly sits on the floor, takes the barman's friend out of his pocket and places it on the carpet. He passes his hands under his buttocks and down past his feet, so that his hands are now in front of him. He stands up, picks up the barman's friend and slowly frees his wrists by carefully cutting the remaining cable tie. Jack is aware he needs to be very careful not to let Amelie know he has managed to free himself. She has a gun, so if she suspected he was no longer shackled it would certainly be curtains for him and that's not the stage variety. He's also aware of what he must do now, he remembers that when Guy was showing him around the Acadian, there was a locker that contained distress flares. If he could manage to get one and set it off, then surely help would arrive, and not even bent cops could stop that from happening. What was it that Amelie had said during her brief phone call with her husband, "You are rowing back?" Well, that would take some time to do if he was rowing back from Dinah Island, wouldn't it? And she's up there waiting for him, so he decides to bite the bullet and go in search of the flares, hoping he will have enough time before Amelie comes back. He goes down a corridor to a locker where he remembers seeing the flares before, he opens the door and there they are, but which one to use as there is quite a selection to choose from.

Chapter 51

SEARCH AND RESCUE

Back on Dinah Island, Ronny has not had much luck in his search for Danny and Mandy, but by some absolute fluke he has stumbled upon the black plastic bag containing the drugs. So, he returns to where he received the gun from Guy excited to tell his co-conspirators of his find, but there is no one to be seen. The tinny's gone and there's no sign of the boss or Tony. Pondering what to do, he decides that he'd better do what his superior, Mr B has directed him to do and resume his search for the runaways and finish them off.

Out in the estuary, Dudley has managed to pull Cherie back into the canoe, but there's no sign of Johnny. They are aware he's a strong swimmer so are certain he's made it to shore, but what if he struck his head when he fell out of the canoe. Cherie is very concerned; she's already found out in the last 24 hours that her husband Declan was killed. Surely fate wouldn't deal her such another cruel blow. She insists that they keep looking for him and Dudley doesn't argue with her. He is manoeuvring the canoe around the estuary with his paddle, while a soaked to the skin Cherie sits up the front keeping an eagle eye out on the water's surface for any sign of her new lost love.

The boss is floundering in the water and is only staying afloat because he is wearing a life preserver. He still has the spear lodged in his right shoulder and is losing a lot of blood but manages to swim in a sideways motion using his left arm in a half backstroke technique to reach the Nudgee Creek shore. He is becoming weak now and is unable to get to his feet.

Johnny has managed to swim back to Dinah Island, determined to get the jump on his pursuers. He is not aware that Cherie was also thrown overboard when the canoe was rammed, so he believes she is perfectly safe with Dudley. He also saw the bald man get hit by Dudley's spear and fall into the water, so is confident that any danger from him has now been dealt with. When he does creep ashore soaking wet, he's surprised to be met by his friend Danny and says, "What the bloody hell are you doing here?" His friends have seen everything that's happened on the estuary and Johnny is quickly taken to where Mandy is in a safe hiding place in the mangroves.

Safely hidden, Danny answers Johnny's question, "The Boudreaux's agreed to bring us here in their yacht, they said they would help us to rescue you."

"Oh really," replies Johnny, "That was nice of them."

"No, not nice at all actually," replies Mandy,

After explaining how they happen to be on Dinah Island as well, one of the first things Danny asks, "Johnny, on Friday night at the Unplugged Cafe did you tell Guy and Amelie anything about the USB that you found in the woods?"

"No," replies Johnny, "I didn't mention it to anyone on Friday night, just Cherie on Saturday. And I only told you on Sunday when we were planning the diversion at Baxter's Jetty. No one else knew anything about the USB, well except the person who broke into my house to steal it back, of course."

"And you wouldn't have mentioned it to the Boudreaux's at any time?"

"No, I haven't had any reason to speak to either of them."

"Then," replies Danny, "I think Guy and Amelie are some kind of drug lords." And he then proceeds to tell him about going to the marina in the early hours of the morning to ask for help and how they agreed for them to use their yacht, but as soon as they stepped onto Dinah Island Guy pulled out a gun and ordered his henchmen to do away with them. He also lets him know that Jack is still on board the yacht, probably unaware of what is taking place.

"They've got Jack?" Johnny is very concerned. "You know, I think that our mate Spud might be mixed up in all this as well, he never responded to my request for help when I asked him to rescue us from the co-op building."

Danny responds in a disappointing tone, "Wow, are you sure Johnny? We were once the Three Musketeers, remember?"

"I know, I know," says Johnny sadly.

Chapter 52

JUMPING JACK FLASH

Back on board the Acadian, Jack is dithering about which flare he should take from the locker. He's trying to remember what Guy told him about them. It was only a quick mention by Guy, so Jack has no idea which one he should select for the purpose of attracting someone to rescue him from this evil witch up on deck, and he doesn't have a clue how to fire one off. So, in frustration he just grabs a couple of large ones and hopes it's the right choice, but when he returns to the salon, Amelie is there waiting for him. He instinctively puts his hands behind his back so she cannot see the flares. She stands there, legs apart, holding the gun in both hands pointing it straight at him, as if she were eyeing a target on a pistol range. "So, you managed to slip out of your cable ties, eh, you are a regular little Houdini, aren't you?"

Jack is flabbergasted, but courageously shouts back, "Shoot me and I will destroy your precious boat."

"Oh, really and how are you going to do that little boy?"

"With these," he holds up the flares, one in each hand.

Amelie is shocked, she knows that a flare in the wrong hands can be a very dangerous fire hazard, and she isn't sure if Jack knows how to use them properly, "I will shoot you before you can do anything," she replies.

"Oh really," shouts Jack, as he clumsily screws the top off one of the flares, which becomes hot in his hand making him jump backwards dropping it onto the floor. At the same time, Amelie fires off a shot at him but misses.

The flare is beginning to spurt out sparks, quickly igniting the salon carpet. Amelie is horrified "Merde!" she shouts in French, "Espece d'idiot!" She fires off another shot at Jack, who is now making his escape by running up the stairs leading onto the deck. Amelie doesn't follow him; she now has only one objective and that is to put out the fire Jack has caused. She needs to get a fire extinguisher quickly and the closest one to hand is kept under the sink in the salon.

Jack is shocked as he bumps into Guy who is coming down the stairs, as he is not aware he's arrived back in the tinny. The collision causes Guy to fall backwards down the stairs and he cries out in pain as he has injured his right arm. Jack arrives on deck with the remaining flare in his left hand, as the palm of his right hand is giving him a slight burning pain from the other flare. Neither Amelie nor Guy have followed him up the stairs, so Jack decides that if he is to be rescued before either of the Boudreaux's finish him off, he needs to act now. He is trying to figure out the instructions on how to utilise the remaining flare and is nervously quoting more Shakespeare, "It's Greek to me." He must fire off this flare because even though black smoke is now coming up out of the salon, which may cause the Acadian to be noticed, he feels he must attract even more attention. He needs to act quickly, so he can save his friends on the island. He looks at the instructions again.

Chapter 53

A NEW LADY OF SHALOTT

Ronny is feeling proud of himself because he's located the drugs, but a little disappointed that he's unable to share his delight with the others. He tried ringing the boss's mobile phone, but there was no answer, so he has now resumed searching for Danny and Mandy on the southern end of Dinah Island as he was ordered to.

Johnny is in hiding with his two friends, but he is drawn from his cover, saying, "Stay here." He leaves them, as he can hear shouting coming from the estuary and spots the Canadian canoe with a lady kneeling at the bow pointing to a dark-suited shape on the Nudgee Beach shore. The dark figure is wearing an orange life preserver with a spear sticking out of him and he's writhing in pain. But this time it is not a dream Johnny is having, there's no Lady of Shallott, or his wife Sophie in the craft, it's Cherie. Her soaking wet body looks magnificent as she gestures with her fists and boldly shouts obscenities at the dark figure. Under Cherie's instructions, Dudley is expertly paddling the canoe as it picks up pace gliding through the water in the direction of the dark figure, ever getting closer and closer to its prey. Similar to a leopard seal coming in for the kill. "Oh, please don't kill him," Johnny is thinking.

As the water becomes shallower and the canoe nears the shoreline, Cherie springs off the craft and into the water, wading at first, then jogging and finally running full pelt towards the boss.

She has built up such a rage inside her as she jumps astride him. The boss feebly holds up his right-hand that Cherie had bitten the night before and it reveals a loose fitted bandage, a handkerchief showing the initials 'M. C-J'. She begins to pummel his head and body with her fists, oblivious to the fact that he is too weak to fight back. She knows this is the man who killed her husband.

Whilst all this has been taking place, Ronny has discovered Danny and Mandy's hiding place and is ushering the couple to come out into the open, while keeping Guy's gun firmly pointing at them. He hasn't even considered that there's someone else nearby, because as far as he's concerned all the others were in the canoe in the estuary, not here. And because Ronny has his back to the water, he is unaware that Johnny is about to rejoin his friends and advise them what is happening at Nudgee Beach. When he sees their predicament, Johnny quickly runs to a spot behind a Pandamus Tree, ensuring he cannot be seen by Ronny, even if he were to now change his position.

Chapter 54

JACK THE LAD

The Acadian still has black smoke billowing out across Moreton Bay, Jack is on deck and has finally managed to work out the instructions and fires off the flare without causing himself any further damage to his right palm. He is ecstatic as he watches the flare reach a high point in the sky and explode like a firework. He is jumping up and down with his arms in the air shouting, "I did it, I did it." At the same moment on hearing the flare, Amelie and Guy emerge from below deck. Amelie's face is blackened, and she is coughing heavily from smoke inhalation and looks a sorry sight with a pistol in hand. She cannot focus properly but manages to fire off a few rounds, missing Jack by a couple of feet. Guy has badly injured his right arm, which is hanging loosely at his side and is probably broken or dislocated. Nevertheless, Jack is in no mood to take any more chances with these two and shimmies himself up the mast, shouting without any fear, "It's time for a wild goose chase," and hangs on for dear life, clinging onto the main sail. Jack now has an excellent view of events happening elsewhere. He notices a traffic chopper has diverted from the Gateway Motorway where it would have been giving traffic reports for morning breakfast shows, and it now seems to be investigating what the flare is all about. The helicopter hovers low over the estuary between Dinah Island and Nudgee Beach and seems more interested in a couple of small craft in that area than the smoke coming from the Acadian. At the same time, two twelve metre XLW Water Police patrol boats are arriving on the scene after leaving their base at Lytton at the mouth of the Brisbane River. One is heading towards the same area where the helicopter is situated, while the other is heading towards the Acadian. And now Jack spots a Volunteer Marine Rescue vessel, an eight-metre Kevlacat 3000 with firefighting equipment on board leaving Cabbage Tree Creek and heading towards the stricken vessel. This makes him feel much happier as he doesn't want to be stuck up there if the fire should escalate.

Chapter 55

THE DYNAMIC DUO
FIGHT BACK

Ronny decides not to shoot Danny and Mandy immediately and leads them back to hopefully reunite with the boss and Tony. His attention is also drawn to a Traffic Chopper flying low over the area. Inspired by seeing Cherie taking revenge on the boss, Johnny sees his chance to overpower a distracted Ronny. He begins charging at him from about twenty metres away, and before Ronny is even aware of his presence, Johnny has crash tackled him to the ground. The force of the tackle knocks the wind out of Ronny causing him to drop his gun, which is quickly retrieved by a relieved Mandy. Danny joins Johnny to restrain a winded Ronny, which they do with some difficulty, as this brute is not going to give up without a fight and a few punches are exchanged.

At the same time, the Water Police patrol boat deposits Sergeant Murphy and P.C. Wilson on the opposite side of the Estuary at Nudgee Beach. They struggle to drag a screaming Cherie off the boss before she can cause him any further damage to what she has already done. After handing over the boss to the Water Police, Sergeant Murphy instructs the young P.C. "Constable, I am handing myself in to you as I have been a corrupt police officer and turned a blind eye to all of this drug smuggling, so I want you to arrest me."

"But sarge, I can't do that," replies the unbelieving constable.

"Yes, you can constable, just read me my rights, you have to do this by the book, go on."

"Well err okay… Sergeant Michael Murphy, you are under arrest, you are charged with the alleged offence of corruption within the police force and aiding and abetting drug smuggling. You do not have to say anything, but anything you do say may be taken down in writing and later used in evidence against you." He takes a deep breath, "How was that sarge?"

"Very good constable, very good." The other uniformed Water Police members are looking on in amazement. "And another thing, constable, I want you to take the pinch for everything today, you know, take the credit for all the other arrests being made here."

"Really sarge? Wow!"

Tony Pesaro, who remained in the dinghy after the ramming does not resist arrest and is in custody as is Ronny who was handed over to them by Danny and Johnny.

The other Water Police patrol boat that went straight to the Acadian, arrived just after the Shorncliffe Volunteer Marine Rescue boat, which after boarding managed to quickly put out the fire in the boat's salon, but it seems to have caused thousands of dollars' worth of damage.

The Water Police helped Jack down from the rigging, and paramedics have treated his burned palm, saying it was only superficial. The Boudreaux's have been put under arrest and Paramedics have diagnosed Guy's arm is broken and put it in a sling and they've given Amelie some oxygen to aid her breathing.

Dudley led the police to where the contraband is hidden as well as showing them where Declan's remains are situated. A forensic team has turned up there to conduct tests and recover the body. After that Dudley simply paddled his canoe back to his home in Lima Street, Nudgee Beach. Later, the fabulous five friends have been reunited on one of the Water Police vessels and taken back to Shorncliffe. The other patrol boat has Tony, Ronny, Guy, Amelie and Mike Murphy in custody, and they are on their way back to the Brisbane River to be processed after dropping off Guy, Amelie and the boss at the Nudgee boat ramp where a couple of ambulances have been waiting to take them to hospitals for some urgent medical attention for their respective injuries sustained.

Chapter 56

EMBARRASSMENT AT SHORNCLIFFE STATION

Danny, Mandy and Jack have been dropped off at the marina to collect the car they left there and although they are tired after their night's ordeal they insist on keeping their promise to take Jack home to Northgate. However, his parents are there waiting to take him home themselves, as they have been trying to find out where he has been for him most of the morning after finding out that he had not slept in his bed on Sunday night, and they are not too happy about what their son might have been involved with. "Jack" says his mother, "What on earth have you been up to, you've been out all night?"

"But mum, I am eighteen you know."

Jack's mother is now starting to fuss over him saying, "Oh Jack, my darling, why is your face is so red and what have you done to your hand?"

"Oh, it's nothing mum," he replies.

Mandy shouts out, "Sorry we've gotten you in trouble Jack."

To which he puts a finger to his lips saying, "Mum's the word."

Mandy looks at Danny raises her eyebrows and says out of the side of her mouth, "That's Shakespeare, isn't it?"

"It certainly is," whispers Danny with a smile.

"You've got a lot of explaining to do when you get home young man" adds his father, "Put your E-scooter in the back and get in the car." Jack just looks at Danny and Mandy, shrugs his shoulders, rolls his eyes and does as his father says.

The Water Police had already dropped Johnny and Cherie off at Baxter's Jetty in Allpass Parade and they are now walking hand in hand towards Jetty Street, tired and exhausted after their weekend's exploits, and looking forward to having a shower, something to eat and getting some sleep as they are both feeling scruffy, famished and completely drained. Many people have gathered along the Shorncliffe shoreline after hearing what's happened in their quiet community and seeing footage from the Traffic chopper on the morning television news programs. Recognising Johnny and Cherie from footage seen; they are being applauded like a bridal couple as they walk past with people saying, "Good on you" and "You beauty," amongst other encouraging remarks. Even the pelicans P1 and P2 are flapping their wings on the shore, as if joining in with the applause. When they arrive at Johnnys' place, Misty is going frantic out the back and Johnny lets her in and gives her some kibble saying, "I don't know what you are complaining about girl, this is all your fault, if you hadn't found that USB then none of this would have happened."

"None of it?" queries Cherie. Then the landline starts to ring and Johnny wondering who it might be picks up saying "Hello?"

It's his daughter Sophie, "Dad, where have you been, I tried to ring you last night to let you know that I was catching a plane this morning, I've tried ringing you again ever since and I've also sent you texts today, but you never answer your mobile. What have you been doing, Dad?"

"Erm… well it's a long story Soppy… sorry Sophie, you see…"

"Dad, you can you tell me when I get there, okay?"

"Oh okay, when does your plane land then?"

"It's already landed Dad, an hour ago, I've caught the air train to Eagle Junction, and now I'm on the Shorncliffe train, so I should be there in about fifteen minutes, can you meet me at the station and help me with my suitcase please?"

"What now? Err… oh, yes, of course, I'm on my way."

"Thanks Dad, see you soon, and I hope you've got a good excuse for not answering your phone."

"Well, yes I think I do have a pretty good one…" Sophie's hung up.

Johnny and Cherie both look quite a sight, they are still wet and covered in mud from their dowsing in the estuary near Nudgee Beach, Cherie is still wearing the capri slacks and AC/DC tee shirt that she borrowed on Sunday morning and they will be in no state to wear again.

"Sorry, but we don't have time for a shower Cherie, we have to get to the station straight away."

"We?" says Cherie looking at herself and not wanting to meet Sophie for the first time looking in such a state.

Johnny is now putting Misty's leash on his dog, "Can't be helped, sorry, come on let's go"

Cherie pleads, "But Johnny, I have mud in my hair," holding out a few strands of matted hair.

"You look fine," he holds out his hand, "Come on, for me, please?"

"Oh, all right, but what is she going to think of me looking like this?" and she reluctantly takes his hand and leaves the house with Johnny and his greyhound.

They decide not to take the car to meet Sophie as their muddy wet state would probably ruin the upholstery, so they walk to the end of Jetty Street, then along Cotton Street and cross Friday Street to Shorncliffe Railway Station, when they hear the first toot of Sophie's train crossing Curlew Street and then the second toot as it crosses Palm Avenue. They arrive at the platform just as the train is pulling into the station and wait for Sophie to emerge.

When Sophie alights from the train with her large suitcase, she is confronted with the sight of a bedraggled couple, wearing dirty, torn and bloodstained clothes with a greyhound by their side and the other departing passengers are giving them strange looks, no applause this time as these people haven't had the opportunity of watching the news yet. Johnny walks up to his daughter gives her a hug and a kiss on the cheek and relieves her of her suitcase saying, "Oh I want you to meet someone" and leading her a few steps "This is Cherie, you might remember her as being in one of Sandcliffe Theatre's plays."

Sophie, who has reacted to her father being soaking wet when he hugged her is now looking at Cherie who to her resembles a destitute refugee from a third-world country, she smiles at her and tentatively holds out her hand whilst whispering in her father's ear, "Dad, why is she wearing my clothes… and what has she done to them?"

"Pleased to meet you" says an embarrassed Cherie, taking Sophie's hand and gently shaking it."

"Let's go home shall we," says Johnny handing Misty's leash to his daughter, he picks up her suitcase, puts a reassuring arm around Cherie and they start walking back to Jetty Street, with Johnny beginning to explain their appearance, "Okay, better let you into what we have been up to the last few days," and proceeds to enlighten his daughter on their weekend adventures.

Chapter 57

READ ALL ABOUT IT

It's Monday night and Johnny, Cherie and Sophie are sitting at the dining room table at Jetty Street, in the middle of a large meal of cod, calamari, battered prawns, scallops and chips accompanied with a glass of white wine. They are watching the six o'clock news which has reports of drug smugglers being apprehended at Shorncliffe in North Brisbane. There is amazing film footage taken from the Traffic chopper showing Ronny who is brandishing a gun at Danny and Mandy when Johnny is seen to emerge from the mangroves and starts running at him giving him a rugby style crash tackle from behind. And there's more footage of Cherie on the shoreline sitting astride the boss, who is wearing an orange life preserver with a spear sticking out of his shoulder and she is pounding him relentlessly with her fists, before the Water Police arrive with Sergeant Murphy and P.C. Wilson on board, who drag her off and arrest the pitiful looking villain. Sophie is amazed saying, "Hey you weren't kidding were you, when you told me you had busted a drug ring, you are both heroes."

The landline rings and Johnny answers laughing, "Hello, hero speaking."

Its Barbara Browning from Plush Agency, "Johnny, I've been trying to ring you on your mobile, why aren't you answering my darling boy?"

"Oh, I lost it in the creek on Sunday night, it has been quite a weekend here you know." He replies calmly.

"Yes, I know, I'm seeing all the reports on the news, you are quite a hero."

"Well, I wouldn't say that, but I'm glad you've called me Barbie. I wanted to let you know there's no way I can make that audition for the pirate movie tomorrow. Firstly, I'm in no fit state and secondly, I haven't had a chance to study the lines or anything, sorry."

"Oh, don't worry about that Johnny, no more support roles for you, it's lead roles only now, all this publicity is fantastic it's just priceless, have you been watching the news this evening?"

"Well yes, I did see some of it," replies Johnny with a big smile on his face.

"It's just perfect advertising for you Johnny, this is going to make you a very hot property, they'll be queueing to sign you up, everyone is going to want you in their movies now."

"Oh, do you really think so?"

"Oh yes I do Johnny and what about that woman who was with you, is she your partner?"

"Well yes I suppose she is, in a way."

"I don't suppose she's done any acting before has she?"

"Well yes," he looks at Cherie," She's a member of the local community theatre company, why?"

"Oh, that's brilliant, just brilliant, look don't let anyone else sign her up, I want her with Plush Agency. We might be able to get you both in a film together and you can be the male and female leads, what do you think about that?"

"Oh, I not sure if she would be interested," says Johnny looking at Cherie again.

"Is she there with you now?"

"Well yes but…"

"But nothing put her on the phone now, I want to speak with her."

Johnny covers the receiver and beckons Cherie to come to the phone, "It's my agent Barbara Browning from Plush Agency, she wants to sign you up, she wants to make you a movie star."

"Me?" giggles Cherie and goes and takes the receiver.

The next morning Johnny and Cherie get a deserved long lie in bed together, but while they were sleeping Sophie and Misty had been out for an early morning walk and she took the opportunity to buy an armful of newspapers. On waking and seeing that they are front page news and the fact that the phone hasn't stopped ringing with offers of TV interviews or magazine articles, they begin to understand what Barbie had told them the day before.

Some of the Tuesday morning newspaper headlines are:
The Australian:
'Community Theatre Brings Curtain Down on Drug Ring'
The Courier Mail:
'Hero Actor Tackles Gang of Drug Smugglers'
The Melbourne Sun:
'Well Known Actor is Real Life Hero'
The Sydney Morning Herald:
'Wonder Woman Makes a Citizen's Arrest'
And even the local **Bayside Star:**
'Shorncliffe Woman Brings Husband's Murderer to Justice'

They were also contacted by all the major TV stations who wanted to do an exclusive special on them. And local radio station, Sangate Sounds fm, got in touch saying that they would like to interview Cherie to promote S.A.T.S. play as she is playing the female lead in 'My Favourite Air Hostess.'

The radio interview with the community radio station went something like this:

"It's Saturday night, welcome to 'Up Late with Larry' on Sandgate Sounds fm Community Radio, I'm your host Languid Larry, good evening. My guest tonight, Cherie O'Bryan is starring in Sandcliffe Amateur Theatre Society's next play a farce called 'My Favourite Air Hostess.' Good evening, Cherie."

"Good evening, Larry, it's nice to be here."

"Now Cherie, before we chat about the play, I couldn't pass up the chance to ask you about the amazing events that occurred in this area a couple of months ago, do you mind?"

"Oh, but you said we would only talk about the play."

"Of course we will, but can I ask you about this first."

Cherie gives Larry the finger.

"Well first of all, this all happened because your partner, well known Australian actor Johnny Blakemore found something when he was walking his dog didn't he?"

"First of all, Larry, he wasn't my partner when he found a USB in the Deagon Wetlands."

"Okay, but he is now, isn't he?"

"Sort of."

"Sort of? Well, is he, or isn't he?"

"Yes, he is now."

"Good, I'm glad we sorted that out. So how did you get involved in all this drug smuggling business then."

"Well, Johnny asked me to help him decipher a code that was on the USB he found."

"And you did manage to break the code, didn't you?"

"Yes, we did."

"And what happened when you worked out the code."

"Can't we just talk about the play, Larry. This was all in the newspapers you know?"

"Yes, I know, but I'd like to hear it from you Cherie."

"We used my kayak to paddle out to Mud Island around midnight on a Saturday night as that was the coordinates that the code identified."

"Okay, and what did you discover there?"

"Erm… drugs Larry, drugs had been dropped off a large ship entering the Port of Brisbane… shouldn't we be promoting S.A.T.S play now Larry?"

"All in good time my dear, and then what happened?"

"Okay Larry I'll keep this as brief as I can, we got chased and I was kidnapped, Johnny rescued me and we ended up on Dinah Island, I found my dead husband, the cops came, they arrested my kidnappers and my husband's killer and we all lived happily ever after, are you happy now?"

"Oh no need to be like that Cherie, well that's all we have time for, back to Late Night with Larry with some music."

Cherie storms out of the studio.

Chapter 58

A FINAL CURTAIN CALL

It's two weeks later and there's a funeral taking place at the Sacred Heart Catholic Church, in Brighton Road, Sandgate. At the altar is a coffin containing Declan O'Bryan's remains and upon the coffin there's a photograph of him holding his daughter Marie, and next to it is a shamrock wreath which has been provided by a group of his old friends and relations who have come all the way from Ireland to attend. All of the Irish visitors are being put up in the homes of Cherie, Johnny and Danny and as per Irish tradition the main wake was held the night before at The Full Moon Hotel in Eagle Terrace. The wake was a lively gathering where mourners drank a lot of the black stuff whilst sharing stories and memories of Declan which was accompanied by Irish songs and music provided by some of the Irish travellers.

At the funeral the priest, Father O'Connor is now saying the final commendation:

"Merciful Lord, turn toward us and listen to our prayers: open the gates of paradise to your servant and help us who remain to comfort one another with assurances of faith, until we all meet in Christ and are with you and with our brother Declan for ever. We ask this through Christ our Lord. Amen."

The congregation all say "Amen."

After the funeral, the coffin is carried down the aisle by four huge pall bearers who are all Declan's Irish relatives and once outside the church, with great respect they carefully position it in the hearse, adjusting the photograph and wreath ready for the journey to the crematorium at the Great Northern Garden of Remembrance. The congregation has been swelled by the Press as the funeral is big news, and photographers from all the main newspapers have been busily snapping photos of anything they think might be newsworthy, but to their credit any journalists there are keeping a respectable distance from the mourners.

A driver is holding open the door of another funeral car and after they are seated, Johnny, whose own wife Sarah's funeral was held at this same church, forgets his painful memories of that day to say to Cherie, "How are you coping with everything?"

"I'm fine thanks, and I'm so grateful that you and Danny have helped with accommodation for everyone that's arrived from overseas, and it's been good of Declan's relatives to come all this way, but I'll be glad when they have all gone back home to Ireland." She sighs, "As for coping with everything, I think that rehearsing for Danny's next play on Sunday afternoons and two nights a week has been very good therapy for me. It's given me lots of other things to concentrate on, like learning lines and working out what clothes to wear for the show, you know things like that."

"Well, I've seen some of those outfits you'll be wearing, there a bit risqué, aren't they?"

She raises her eyebrows, "Well, I never took you for a prude Johnny." They sit back and hold hands smiling at each other as their black limousine follows slowly behind the hearse.

It's six weeks later, and there's a packed audience at the beautiful Sandgate Town Hall watching an afternoon matinee of the final performance of Sandcliffe Amateur Theatre Society's play 'My Favourite Air Hostess.' It was almost impossible for regular patrons to buy a ticket for the opening night performance as most of the seats were purchased by eager journalists looking for a side story to the drug smugglers. And there was no need on this occasion to provide freebie tickets to all those self-important reviewers looking to see a free show and have a free supper afterwards. There were also a few photographers who had turned up to take photos for their newspapers who left very disappointed when they were turned away and told they were not allowed to take photographs or make any recordings of any kind of the show as it would infringe the play's copyright rules.

In what was a rarity for the theatre group, all the play's performances have sold out, including the balcony seats, which required SATS to put on two weekends of extra shows to satisfy demand. That was mainly down to the publicity gained from their lead actress, Cherie who is now a local hero. As mentioned, she had that disastrous interview with Languid Larry on Sounds of Sandgate FM community radio, which will probably be the last time SATS will be invited on again, but no money changed hands for that. Any money made from interviews with the major TV networks by the famous five as they have been nicknamed (Dudley refused to be interviewed) has all been donated back to the Sandcliffe Theatre, who have also made a small fortune out of merchandise sales, SATS. caps and Tee shirts being the most popular items purchased, so their finances are in pretty good shape.

Johnny is sitting in the front row watching the play with Sophie, Jack, Dudley and his wife Jayd and Colby's son Michael who has returned from overseas with his new gorgeous Swedish girlfriend Annalisa after hearing of the events on Dinah Island, which was worldwide news. The Smith sisters, Millie and Tillie are also there sitting up on the balcony, dressed in identical outfits and towards the back of the auditorium are Marcel and Bonnie or should we say Dee Jay, Languid Larry and his partner. Everyone seems to be having a good time and enjoying the show.

On stage, the set is the living room of an apartment, and Cherie has just come out of a bedroom looking amazing in a revealing negligee and wearing a platinum-coloured pageboy-style wig and she is now clinging onto Danny, who is sporting a dapper moustache for his role, and his trousers are down around his ankles. Mandy, who is playing Danny's wife in the play is also scantily clad, and sporting a new perm, especially for the role. She enters through another bedroom door shouting "Ah ha, caught you both in the act." The chimes of the Town Hall clock signify the time is 4:30pm as the bright red curtains slowly close to rapturous applause, and a few seconds later reopen again to allow all the actors to take their well-deserved bows one after the other to even more sustained applause. Especially from Johnny and his daughter who are both standing in appreciation.

"Did you enjoy it?" Johnny asks his daughter.

"Yes Dad, she's marvellous, it's about time you found someone again, I'm so happy for you."

"Thank you, Sophie." He kisses her gently on the forehead.

Afterwards, all the cast come out into the foyer to interact with the audience, and everyone agrees that it has been a successful run. There is only one embarrassing moment when the Smith sisters tell Cherie that they are glad she has recovered from her migraines to which Johnny quickly says to a confused Cherie, "I'll explain later."

That evening members of S.A.T.S. and invited guests are having an after-show party in a private room at Shorncliffe's historic Seaview Hotel, built in the 1870's and located in Pier Street, opposite St Pat's College. The press has been banned from this function and the hotel have taken it upon themselves to hire a heavily built security man to ensure that there are no unwanted intruders.

All close friends and relatives are sitting around a large table, each enjoying their favourite beverage and listening to music provided by a Dee Jay. At the other end of the room, Marcel and Bonnie, that is Languid Larry and his partner, can be seen standing close together in front of the Dee Jay and swaying to the music. When Cherie finds out they're there and that they must have snuck in as they were not invited, she discretely requests the security man to eject them, which he promptly does, much to Larry's disgust, who says loudly, "No more free promos for you," as he leaves.

Michael has introduced all those around the table to his girlfriend Annalisa, who speaks exceedingly good English. Everyone has been talking about the show, with Jack commenting, "It was so good one laughed oneself into stitches."

"No more Shakespeare!" all the others plead.

The discussion at the table quickly turns to the events of the weekend in early July. "So, Dudley, did the police give you your spear back yet?" asks Johnny.

Dudley just shrugs, "Not yet I'm afraid, they need it for evidence, but they decided not to prosecute me for assault with a deadly weapon and agreed it was self-defence."

"They should be awarding you with a medal Dudley," responds Cherie, "But you know, if it was me who had thrown that spear, I wouldn't have wounded him I would have got him right through the heart." She does the motion of throwing a spear.

"So, the mysterious man in black did survive then?" asks Danny.

"Yes unfortunately," Cherie replies with a little bitterness.

"Anyway, do we know who he is?" adds Danny.

"Yes, we do know," confirms Johnny. "That handkerchief that we found near Declan's body had the initials 'M. C-J.' on it. His name is Miles Cleaver-Jones, from London, I think he's wanted in the U.K. as well. Tony Pesaro decided to come clean and tell the cops everything he knew by confirming Miles Cleaver-Jones shot Declan and stuffed a handkerchief into his mouth. It didn't take long for Divers to recover the gun he dropped in the estuary near Nudgee Beach and forensics have matched it to the bullet that was used to kill Declan. Anyway, he's going away for a very long time, because there's no doubt at all he's the murderer, and no way he'll get away with it."

"What about the others?" enquires Mandy.

Johnny continues, "Well, Tony's also put the finger on Ronny Carter for causing the drowning of Manfred Muller, you know, the German crew member. So, Ronny will go down for murder as well."

"And what punishment do you think Tony Pesaro will get?" asks Mandy sipping her wine.

"Well, because he's cooperated fully with the police, he will most likely get a much-reduced sentence and only be charged for his involvement in drug trafficking."

"And for holding me hostage" insists Cherie.

"Oh yes, that as well," confirms Johnny.

"Speaking of the police, what's going to happen to your old friend Sergeant Mike Murphy," asks Dudley.

"Well, he was only a minor part in all this" says Johnny, "But he will have to spend some time inside of course, as he did turn a blind eye to everything that went on. He didn't mention in a report that the car I saw at the scene of the bashing was a blue commodore, which turned out to belong to the German who was murdered. And he ignored my phone message for help to rescue Cherie from the co-op building."

"And I'd bet that he didn't even bother investigating Declan's disappearance, when I asked him to. As he already knew he had been killed," adds Cherie.

"They will be devastated at St. Pats to hear that an old boy has been convicted of crimes and sent to prison," adds Danny. "His career is well and truly over now of course, but to his credit his conscience did make him do the right thing in the end."

"That's True," says Johnny. "And hasn't another former St Pats student P.C. Wilson done well for himself; I've heard there's a chance he may be promoted to Detective Constable soon."

Danny raises his glass, "And they will also be proud that an old boy who used to play for St Pats First XV made such a tremendous rugby tackle to floor one of the criminals, Johnny?" he takes a swig of his beer.

"Yeah, maybe," replies Johnny modestly.

"I'm still getting over the shock of Sandcliffe Theatre's main patrons, the Boudreaux's being involved in all this," interjects Jack, whose right hand has now completely healed after being burned by the flare.

"Yes, I've been thinking about them," says Danny. "Remember when I bumped into Guy that Friday, and I invited him to the Unplugged Café evening?" They all nod. "Well, I reckon he already knew about your dog Misty, accidentally finding the USB, so he jumped at the chance to come along and try and find out more, and also, so he could keep an eye on you Johnny, while the bald man was breaking into your house."

"And they dropped themselves right in it didn't they, when Amelie mentioned the USB at the marina, and none of us had spoken to them about it previously," says Jack.

Mandy adds, "And do you recall that both Guy and Amelie left the Unplugged Café early that night, it was right after the bald man in the black suit had poked his head in? I think they wanted to go outside to see him and make sure that he'd got the USB back."

"Yes, you're probably right about that Mandy" says Cherie joining in the conversation again. "Unfortunately, the Boudreaux's have refused to cooperate with the police at all, so they are not going to be able to prosecute anyone higher up in that drug cartel, but Guy and Amelie will get done for their involvement in drug trafficking and for being accessories to murder as well, not to mention holding you hostage Jack."

"Yeh, but they took on more than they bargained for, didn't they? I soon sorted them out." says Jack who is thumping his chest, Tarzan style.

Johnny smiles at Jack saying, "They must have thought they were so lucky when you three arrived in the middle of the night asking for help, but I bet they wish you hadn't turned up now. If you hadn't, they might have got away Scot free and sailed away to another part of the world."

Jack smiles smugly. "Yeah, but they are not going to be able to use that yacht for quite some time, are they?"

"Anyway, changing the subject slightly" Danny is proposing a toast, "I would like you all to raise your glasses and toast Cherie on a wonderful performance tonight. We are in great appreciation of her for honouring her roll in Sandcliffe Theatre's farce, 'My Favourite Air Hostess,' especially now that she is so famous, and I believe a very hot property and I'm not talking real estate." He raises his glass saying, "So here's to Cherie!"

"Hear, hear!" Jack shouts and they all raise their glasses and say, "To Cherie!" in unison.

Cherie is blushing. "Well, let's see what happens, shall we," and knocks back her wine. "Anyway, it's time to party!" She regains her composure and hurries onto the dance floor, dragging

Johnny with her, as the DJ has just started playing The Fine Young Cannibals song 'Johnny Come Home' and the others quickly join them. Danny and Mandy, their son Michael and Annalisa, followed by Dudley and Jayd and not to be outdone, Jack asks Sophie up on the dance floor as well. Even the Smith sisters, who have been sitting very quietly in a corner sipping at their sherries decide to get up and join in the dancing.

Later, outside the Seaview Hotel, everyone had a good time, so they said their farewells with lots of hugs and kisses. Then, Johnny and Cherie wave to Sophie who drives off in Johnny's car she is borrowing as she's staying with friends nearby. Our couple begin walking down Yundah Street on their way to their home in Jetty Street because Cherie has moved in with him now. She says, "You know, I think I might give this acting lark a try, what do you think?"

Johnny stops walking and gives her a hug, "Why not, I think that's a great idea, and Barbie can't wait to sign you up with Plush Agency and get you some roles, especially now that you've finished this play."

"Okay then, I'm a bit over real estate anyway, it seems so boring after all we've been through, I'll give Barbie a ring in the morning." She looks at Johnny, "Has she managed to find you anything yet?"

"Oh, there's a couple of things on the horizon, but I am happy to concentrate on other things at the moment."

"Like what, may I ask?"

"Well, you of course," they embrace and kiss passionately. "And I have another project I want to spend some time on as well."

"Which is?"

"I have a novel in mind, I'm thinking of calling it 'The Cabbage Tree Creek Caper' what do you think?"

"Sounds just perfect!"

The End.